Alien Genocide

The Tactical Advantage Series – Book One

Sean Patrick Posey

You can see other titles I have available on my website:

seanpatrickposey.com

ACKNOWLEDGEMENTS

For Nicole, my sweet, beautiful, loving wife who encouraged me to write this book, and for my sweet beautiful daughters Alyssa and Sarah for whom I would do anything. I love you all.

Special thanks to my older brother Mark Posey and his wife Tracy Cooper-Posey for the help they gave me in writing and publishing this book. Tracy is an experienced author and gave me a ton of advice on writing the book, making my cover, and the publishing process. They have been through this whole process many times and their advice made things a lot easier for me. You can see all of Tracy's books on her website: **tracycooperposey.com**

TABLE OF CONTENTS

PROLOGUE

The year is 2165, eighty-five years since scientists on Earth created the first crude FTL (faster than light) drive, allowing us to travel out into the galaxy. Shortly after venturing out into space, we discovered we were not alone in the universe.

We came across other species in our travels, some that were friendly and some that were not. Many of the friendly species traded with us and helped us develop more advanced technology.

This new technology allowed us to travel faster and farther. It allowed us to build bigger, more powerful spaceships with advanced weapons and shields to defend ourselves against the aggressive species.

Knowing we were not alone in the universe drastically changed things on Earth. Whenever there was an extraterrestrial threat, or an actual conflict, the people of Earth pulled together, showing unity and strength to whatever species was being aggressive towards us.

Eventually, the United Nations evolved into the World Council which governed over Earth's extraterrestrial relations.

One of the first things the new World Council did was to create a new military entity charged with protecting Earth and its interests from external threats. This military entity was aptly named the Earth Defense Force or EDF.

To keep the peace, protect our citizens, and uphold the laws internally, the World Council created Earth's Planetary Police Force.

Although many things have evolved and changed, society is still plagued with a criminal element which is compounded by the alien factor.

CHAPTER 1 - THE LAST MISSION

Admiral Nathan Stone is awakened by the gentle sounds of a Zen melody. He opens his eyes, rolls over and touches the glass touch panel top of his nightstand. The touch panel illuminates, a holographic display appears above the nightstand displaying the ship's status, the Zen melody stops playing, and the lights in his state room power up slowly to a gentle yellowish hue, just enough to see without hurting his eyes.

He throws the covers off, sits up, and puts his feet on the floor. He yawns, stretches, rubs his face with his hands, and then stands up and walks into his bathroom. He begins his day the same way he has every day since he was promoted to admiral and given command of Earth's flagship five years ago.

This morning feels different however, as it's his last day of active military duty. He is retiring after twenty-five years of service. Every person in the military faces this day. For Nathan, the only life he has known since he was eighteen years old, is about to change drastically.

He steps into the shower and drops his head under the stream of hot water. After mere seconds, he is deep in thought, his mind taking him in all directions. A stroll down memory lane, reliving past adventures and wondering what adventures are to come. Through all of these thoughts, the question that keeps repeating in his mind is, "Am I doing the right thing?"

With his mind obsessively occupied, pondering his decision and his future, he loses track of time. He suddenly realizes half an hour has passed, and he is now running late. He quickly finishes up and turns the water off.

After his shower, he finds himself deep in thought once again. Staring himself in the eyes in the mirror, his face lathered up, razor in hand, looking for an answer to his question. An answer that never comes. After snapping out of it, he finishes his morning routine, gets dressed in his navy-blue uniform and heads toward the door. As he approaches, the gray, metal door slides open, but instead of walking through he pauses at the threshold. He turns and looks around his state room for a minute, his home for the last five years, then turns back and walks out. The door slides closed behind him.

It's still early morning on the ship and the admiral doesn't pass anyone in the corridor on the way to his private dining room. When he enters, he is greeted by his chef who has made him his favorite breakfast, west coast eggs benedict.

"Thank you, Chef, this looks delicious as always."

"You're very welcome, Admiral, and may I say it has been both a pleasure and an honor cooking for you for the last five years."

The admiral shakes his hand and replies with a smile, "The honor and pleasure were mine, and thank you for everything."

The admiral sits down to eat while he reviews the night watch commander's logs in a holographic display projected from the center of his dining table. When he finishes eating, he grabs a large black coffee and heads for the bridge.

The walk to the elevator seems a little different this morning, things that he has taken for granted for the last five years are grabbing his full attention. Each computer console, light, hatch and bulkhead are jumping out at him. He even notices the feel and vibration of the deck plates under his feet just as he did five years ago when he took command.

When he reaches the elevator, the doors open, he steps in and pushes the button for the bridge. The doors close and the elevator begins rise. When the elevator stops, the doors open, the admiral steps out and turns to his left. As he approaches the bridge, the ship's computer identifies him and automatically opens the two large, thick, glass and steel doors that secure the command deck of the ship.

The admiral stands just outside the open bridge doors for a minute taking in the high-tech beauty of the ship's command center. Most of the bridge is adorned in a gloss white polycarbonate with some medium blue accents. There are also transparent section dividers and railings throughout the bridge. There are high-tech displays and touch screen control consoles at every station. All the displays and touch screen consoles have a high gloss black background with the control interfaces displayed in a medium to light blue color palette. There are several projected holographic displays operating throughout the bridge, including one at the tactical station and one at the navigation station. There is a combination of highly ergonomic, very comfortable, molded, seated stations that are manned continuously, and a few standing stations that are not. The outer bridge walls have a number of ten-foot-high by seven-foot-wide window sections, which have provided some spectacular views over the years. At the front of the bridge is a large view screen that retracts into the floor when not in use. The design and color combination of the bridge truly is a thing of beauty.

After a few minutes, the admiral snaps back to reality and steps onto the bridge.

As he steps foot on the bridge, the ship's computer announces in its female voice, "Admiral on deck."

Everyone on the bridge immediately stands and snaps to attention.

The admiral walks over to the command chair and sits down.

"At ease, everyone."

Everyone takes their station again.

"Chief of the Watch, status report."

"Aye sir, it was a quiet night. The ship is on course traveling at 14 TSL, all systems are green, and we will reach the rendezvous point in approximately thirty minutes."

"Thank you, Chief."

The admiral sits there quietly sipping his coffee and watching the stars streak by for about fifteen minutes.

He then checks his watch and says, "XO, sound battle stations."

"Aye sir."

The XO grabs the microphone and announces over the ship's address system, "Battle stations, battle stations, all hands man your battle stations, this is not a drill."

An alarm sounds after his address and the lights on the bridge change from white to red.

A minute later he says, "Admiral, all sections report battle stations manned and ready."

"Thank you, XO."

"Tactical, shields up, full power in reflective mode. Bring the holo-projectors and the cloaking device online and run program Envoy One."

"Aye sir, shields up, full power in reflective mode. Bringing the holo-projectors and the cloaking device online now. Running program Envoy One."

"Thank you, Tactical."

The bridge is quiet for several more minutes until the helmsman says, "Admiral, we are one minute away from the edge of Earth's space and the rendezvous point."

"Thank you, Helm."

A minute later the admiral says, "Helm, drop us out of FTL."

"Aye sir."

The crew sees a bright blue flash of light through the bridge windows as the ship drops out of FTL.

Instantly, a beautiful star field and a large multi-colored nebula appear through the bridge windows and on the large main view screen.

"Tactical, scan this sector of space for any other ships."

"Aye sir, scanners show there are no other ships in the area."

"Thank you, Tactical."

"Helm, all stop."

"Aye sir, the helm is answering all stop."

"Tactical, change the bridge lighting back to standard."

"Aye sir."

The lights change from red back to white.

"That's better, we don't want to alarm the Sulari when they arrive."

Several minutes go by, the bridge is quiet with just the standard operational chatter over the comm systems.

Then an electronic warning bell chimes, and a red light flashes on the tactical officer's console.

"Admiral, there are three ships approaching our position in FTL."

The admiral shifts forward in his chair and focuses his attention on the main view screen. He doesn't have to wait for long, as the three ships drop out of FTL and come to a full stop about two kilometers off the port bow.

The admiral uses the command console on his chair to magnify the main view screen so he can get a better look at the ships. They are large, dark, menacing looking ships that appear to be heavily armed.

"Comms, hail the Sulari vessels and request they communicate visually with us."

The communications officer says, "Aye sir," pushes a button on her headset and says in a very polite tone, "Attention, Sulari vessels, this is Earth Envoy One. Admiral Stone requests you communicate visually with us."

A few seconds later she says, "Admiral, I have received a response."

"Thank you, Comms, on screen."

"Aye sir."

A few seconds later the main view screen switches from displaying the three ships to displaying the bridge of one of the Sulari ships with their captain sitting in his chair, front and center. The Sulari are hideous, reptilian looking creatures, whose faces resemble that of a large bullfrog, but even uglier if that is possible.

The admiral stands up, takes a few steps towards the view screen and says in a diplomatic tone, "Greetings, I'm Admiral Nathan Stone of the Earth Defense Force."

The Sulari captain replies, "Greetings, Admiral Stone, I'm Captain Verkusk Creeksto of the Sulari vessel Croixa."

"It's a pleasure to meet you, Captain Creeksto."

"The pleasure is all mine, Admiral Stone."

"Captain, your request for this meeting was more than a little vague so tell me, what can we do for you?"

"We require passage through Earth's space to a little planet called Trynx 3, Admiral."

"May I ask the reason you need passage to Trynx 3?"

"I'm afraid that I am not at liberty to say, Admiral."

The admiral raises one eyebrow and says, "You're not at liberty to say? I'm sorry Captain, but I can't accept that answer. I need to know the reason you wish to visit a planet in the center of Earth's sector of space."

Captain Creeksto repeats, "I'm sorry, Admiral, but I am not at liberty to say."

"Then I'm sorry, Captain, but I must refuse you passage through Earth's space."

Captain Creeksto's face changes to a darker shade of green and in a raised voice he says, "Admiral Stone, you are hardly in a position to refuse us passage. We have three, large, heavily armed warships and your puny ship appears to be unarmed. What's stopping us from destroying your ship and going to Trynx 3, anyway?"

With a slight grin on his face, the admiral sits back down in his chair and says, "I wouldn't try that if I were you, Captain."

Everyone on the bridge of the Sulari ship bursts out in laughter, including Captain Creeksto.

When the laughter dies down Captain Creeksto says, "Come now, Admiral, there is no need for you to die today. Clearly, your ship is no match for ours. I can't believe that an admiral in the Earth Defense Force has such a tiny little ship. It's almost insulting for you to even try to bluff us like this when you obviously don't hold any cards."

The admiral smiles a little more and says, "You shouldn't rely on your eyes alone, Captain."

He hits a button on the command console on his chair to cut off communication with the Sulari ship.

"Tactical, take the holo-projectors and the cloaking device offline."

"Aye sir, taking the holo-projectors and the cloaking device offline now."

On the Sulari ship the main view screen cuts from viewing the Earth ship's bridge to an exterior image. The small Earth ship slowly fades out and disappears as the holo-projectors disengage.

The smug smile disappears from Captain Creeksto's face and is soon replaced by a look of shock and fear as the cloaking device disengages and the pride of Earth's fleet, the battle carrier Invincible, fades into view. The massive battle carrier dwarfs the Sulari ships, at a little over a mile and a half long, two-thirds of a mile wide, and a third of a mile high, it dwarfs any known ship in the galaxy.

Captain Creeksto notices that a great number of the Earth ship's huge laser cannons are trained on his ships and that they have already launched at least three full squadrons of fighters that seem to be waiting patiently in attack formation, about one hundred meters above the flight deck.

Back on the Invincible the admiral says, "That's probably long enough for the shock to wear off. Comms, hail them again."

The communications officer says, "Aye sir," presses a button on her headset and with just a touch of indignation in her voice says, "Captain Creeksto, this is the Earth Defense Force battle carrier Invincible…, Admiral Stone would like to speak to you again."

A few seconds later she says, "Admiral, I have received a response."

"Thank you, Comms, on screen."

"Aye sir."

Captain Creeksto's hideous face once again appears on the large main view screen.

With a slightly smug look on his face the admiral says, "Well, Captain, as you can see my ship is not as puny and defenseless as you thought. The way I see it, you have two choices, you can attack and be killed, or you can leave peacefully, the choice is yours."

Captain Creeksto realizing that he has been outsmarted says, "Well played, Admiral Stone, well played."

"I never go into any situation without a tactical advantage, Captain, you may want to keep that in mind."

Captain Creeksto says, "Until next time, Admiral," and then closes the channel.

The Sulari ships again appear on the main view screen and the bridge crew of the Invincible watches as they turn and move off. After about a minute the Sulari ships enter FTL and disappear in bright blue flashes of light.

"CAG, bring the fighters home."

"Aye sir."

The CAG presses a button on his headset and says, "Attention, all fighters, this is the CAG speaking, bring 'em home."

"XO, stand down from battle stations."

"Aye sir."

The XO grabs the microphone and announces over the ship's address system, "All hands, this is the XO. Stand down from battle stations, repeat stand down from battle stations."

The admiral gets up out of his chair and walks over to the port side bridge windows overlooking the flight deck. He looks up and watches the three squadrons of fighters peel off and circle around behind the carrier to land.

He smiles and thinks to himself, "Oh to be a fighter pilot again," and then walks back over to his chair and sits down.

After about twenty minutes the CAG says, "Admiral, all fighters are back on board."

"Thank you, CAG."

"Navigator, set course for Earth."

"Aye sir, course laid in."

"Helm, come about, one hundred and eighty degrees. When you've completed your turn engage the FTL drive, speed 14 TSL."

"Aye sir, coming about, one hundred and eighty degrees."

When the massive battle carrier has completed the turn, it accelerates away rapidly. The bridge crew sees a bright blue flash of light through the bridge windows as the ship passes the speed of light.

A minute later the helmsman says, "Admiral, we have reached 14 TSL and are on course for Earth."

"Thank you, Helm."

The admiral sits back in his chair watching the stars streak by the bridge windows for a few minutes and then he gets up and heads towards the large bridge doors.

The doors open as he approaches them and he says, "XO, you have the con. I'll be in my state room packing my things."

"Aye sir, I have the con."

The admiral leaves the bridge and the large doors close behind him.

The Invincible arrives back at Earth early the next morning and the admiral is awake early to finish packing. He piles the boxes containing his belongings beside the door, along with instructions to ship them to his home just outside Jasper, Alberta in the Canadian Rocky Mountains.

Following Navy tradition, he is wearing his white dress uniform, the left side of his chest covered in ribbons, medals and commendations.

Before leaving his state room for the last time, he pauses to take one last look around before he dons his white dress cover and heads towards the door.

As he nears the door, it slides open and to his surprise the corridor outside his state room is lined on both sides with officers and crew members all in their dress white uniforms. His executive officer is the first man outside the door on the right-hand side of the corridor.

The XO yells, "ATTENTION ON DECK!"

Everyone in the corridor snaps to attention.

It's really no surprise that so many of the crew lined up to bid the admiral farewell as he was always very respected and popular with the entire crew aboard the Invincible.

Over the PA speakers sounds a Bosun's whistle, piping the notes to signify that the commanding officer is leaving the ship. When the third pitch is played on the whistle, everyone in the corridor salutes, their hands remaining up at the side of their foreheads.

The admiral walks out into the corridor looking straight ahead. As the admiral passes, the executive officer finishes his salute and follows behind the admiral escorting him to the shuttle bay. They walk past hundreds of officers and crew members all dressed in their whites on their way to the elevator.

The XO accompanies the admiral in the elevator down to the battle carrier's internal tram system. The two officers board the waiting tram which then speeds off to shuttle bay alpha. When the tram arrives at the shuttle bay, the admiral can see more saluting crew members dressed in their white uniforms lined up on either side of the pathway from the tram to the waiting shuttle. The two officers exit the tram and walk past all the crew members to the waiting shuttle where they turn and face each other, salute each other and shake hands.

"XO, it has been both an honor and a privilege."

"The honor and privilege were mine, Admiral."

The admiral smiles at the XO and then steps aboard the shuttle, the door closing behind him.

The XO turns to face all the crew members still standing at attention and still saluting.

He yells, "DIS-MISSED!"

The crew finish their salutes, then turn and file out of the shuttle bay.

Inside the shuttle the Admiral takes a seat and tells the pilot he is ready to go.

The elevator the shuttle is on rises towards the flight deck, the atmospheric force field activates, and the large doors open above them.

As the shuttle rises through the flight deck, the admiral can see the island superstructure to his right. He admires the sheer size of the ship and realizes how much he will miss her.

The shuttle pilot gets clearance from Invincible's air traffic control to depart, so the shuttle lifts off the deck and turns to head towards the planet. The admiral looks back at the massive battle carrier as they descend into the atmosphere.

CHAPTER 2 - THE RETIREMENT BALL

Admiral Stone's shuttle touches down at the Earth Defense Force fleet headquarters in Seattle, Washington at approximately 09:30 hours Pacific standard time. When the shuttle door opens, the fleet marching band starts playing, and two enlisted men in their dress white uniforms, roll a red carpet up to the shuttle.

As the admiral steps out of the shuttle door, he sees the red carpet rolled out before him leading to a small stage where the Secretary of the Fleet, Admiral Michael Hollister, and Fleet Admiral, Timothy Daniels, await him. Lining the sides of the red carpet and surrounding the stage are a couple of hundred officers and enlisted men in their dress white uniforms standing at attention.

Admiral Stone steps down from the shuttle and the instant his feet hit the ground, everyone present, except for Admiral Hollister and Admiral Daniels, salute him. Admiral Stone returns their salute, walks up the red carpet and on to the stage where he turns to face Admiral Hollister and Admiral Daniels. He then stands at attention and salutes them. Admirals Hollister and Daniels return his salute, they all shake hands and exchange pleasantries. The band stops playing as the brief ceremony starts, to hand over command of the Invincible.

Admiral Hollister yells out, "ADMIRAL ROBERT JAMESON FRONT AND CENTER!"

Admiral Jameson walks over from the side of the stage and turns to face admirals Hollister and Daniels. He then stands at attention and salutes them. Admirals Hollister and Daniels return his salute, then they all shake hands and exchange pleasantries. Admiral Jameson then turns to face Admiral Stone. Admirals Stone and Jameson salute each other and shake hands.

Admiral Jameson says, "Admiral Stone, I relieve you."

Admiral Stone replies, "Admiral Jameson, I stand relieved."

Admirals Stone and Jameson salute each other and then turn to face turns to face admirals Hollister and Daniels. Admirals Stone and Jameson salute admirals Hollister and Daniels. Admirals Hollister and Daniels return their salute.

An officer at the end of the stage yells, "DIS-MISSED!"

All the officers and enlisted men lining the red carpet and surrounding the stage finish their salutes and disperse. Some just walk away from the proceedings some wait around to shake Admiral Stone's and Admiral Jameson's hands to congratulate them.

When the crowd has dispersed, there is a junior officer waiting for Admiral Stone to escort him to a car that's waiting to take him to his hotel. The officer informs Admiral Stone that the banquet and ball for his retirement will be held at the fleet headquarters grand ballroom that night and that a limousine will pick him up from the hotel at 18:30 hours. Admiral Stone thanks the officer, they salute each other, the admiral gets in the back seat of the car and the car drives off.

When Admiral Stone arrives at the hotel, he checks in and heads up to his suite, the penthouse suite. When he enters the suite, he walks right over to the French doors to the terrace, opens them up, walks out, leans on the railing and admires the view of the city. He spends the rest of the day in the suite relaxing and polishing up his speech.

At about 17:00 hours someone knocks on the hotel door. He answers it to find a porter with a garment bag in hand. The admiral thanks him, takes the bag, tips him and closes the door. The admiral takes the bag into the bedroom, drops it on the bed and opens it to find his tuxedo uniform all pressed and ready for his big night. He pulls his tuxedo out of the bag and lays it neatly on the bed, after which he hangs the empty bag in the closet.

He looks at his watch and decides it's time for a drink, so he wanders over to the bar, pours himself a rather generous twenty-one-year-old single malt scotch, walks back into the bedroom and gets ready for the night.

When the admiral is ready, he heads down to the lobby to wait for the limousine that will take him to the ball. When he steps out of the elevator, he sees there are quite a number of people in the lobby and he notices that a lot of them turn to look at him, especially the women.

Admiral Stone is a very attractive, tall man with a muscular build, dark brown hair and blue eyes. His looks combined with the fact that he is wearing a white tuxedo uniform with a chest full of ribbons, commendations and medals, elicits a lot of attention from the opposite sex.

The limousine picks him up out front of the hotel at 18:30 hours and takes him back to fleet headquarters. Upon exiting the limousine, he is met by the event coordinator, a rather beautiful, tall, blonde woman dressed in an exotic and revealing, little, black dress.

She smiles, looks him up and down and says, "Good evening, Admiral Stone, I'm Heather McMillan, the event coordinator."

Due to the revealing nature of her dress, Nathan can't help but check her out before smiling and saying, "Pleased to meet you, Heather."

She takes his right hand and says, "If you come with me, Admiral, I will lead you to the grand ballroom."

As the admiral and the event coordinator enter the grand ballroom, hundreds of people swiftly stand up and applaud. The admiral is blown away by the number of people in attendance to wish him well as he leaves the military.

The grand ballroom is a typical ballroom with a head table at the front, a dance floor in front of that and a bunch of round tables for the guests to sit at. The lighting is subdued except for the bright spotlight that targeted the admiral as soon as he walked in.

The event coordinator escorts the admiral to the head table where he shakes the hands of all the officers and dignitaries that have come to honor him tonight including admirals Hollister and Daniels.

When the admiral finishes greeting everyone at the head table, he turns to take his seat and spots a very familiar face standing at the podium, his best friend Carter Rayburn. They grew up together and served in the military together until about five years ago when Carter left the military to join Earth's Planetary Police Force.

The admiral walks over to his best friend, gives him a big hug and says, "Hey old buddy, it's great to see you, thanks for coming."

Carter smiles, puts his hand on his shoulder and says, "It's great to see you too, but I'm not just here to celebrate your retirement my friend. I'm the master of ceremonies for this little shin dig, or maybe calling it a roast at this point would be more appropriate."

Laughing, Carter walks away from his best friend, leaving him with a shocked look on his face.

Carter walks over to the podium, grabs the microphone and says, "Good evening everyone, would you all please take your seats so we can get started?"

Once everybody has taken a seat and quieted down, he says, "Good evening everyone. My name is Carter Rayburn and I am your master of ceremonies for the evening. I am also Admiral Stone's best friend so naturally it's my duty to tell you a little about him, and to embarrass him as much as possible," after which the crowd laughs.

The admiral smiles, looks down, and shakes his head slightly as if to say, "Oh crap, fasten your seatbelts. It's going to be a wild ride."

Carter continues, "I first met Nathan Stone when he and I were five years old. We grew up together, we went to school together, played sports together, trained in the martial arts together, went to the academy together and we served together."

"Most of the people in this room know that Nathan Stone is the youngest officer promoted to the rank of admiral in the history of any of Earth's militaries. He is a brilliant tactician who pioneered most of the fleet's tactics used today, he has nerves of steel, he is well liked and respected by his superiors and by the people that have served under him."

"While all of that is true today, I can remember a time when things were a little different. For instance, I remember one occasion at the academy when then Cadet Stone was up all night partying and fell asleep in class the next morning."

"He was asleep when our instructor announced that the next morning, we would get our first supersonic ride in an F-98 exo-fighter. The instructor told us we would be going up, with some of their most experienced pilots, in two seat trainers and that they would push us, twist us and turn us to see if we could handle the high g-forces fighter pilots experience. The instructor also warned us to skip breakfast that morning if we were smart."

The crowd laughs and Carter looks over at his friend and sees him with his face in his hands, shaking his head slightly, but even with his face covered Carter could tell he was laughing.

"And I know as his best friend, I should have told him what was going to happen the next day, and about the warning our instructor had given us, but the little devil on my shoulder said, 'NAH.' So, the next morning I made sure that he had a big breakfast consisting mostly of scrambled eggs."

The crowd groans and starts laughing again. Once again Carter looks over at his friend and sees he is now sitting back in his chair and is looking at Carter with a look on his face that says, "Oh, I am so going to get you for this."

Fighting laughter Carter says, "So when we sat down in class and the instructor told us to go get in our flight gear, I looked over at him and smiled. He looked back at me with just a hint of anger in his eyes and said, 'You son of a bitch.' He couldn't be too angry with me though because he knew that if the situation were reversed, he would have done the exact same thing to me," the crowd laughs again.

"I'll spare you the gory details, but his breakfast only stayed down until the second high-speed turn. Funny enough he never fell asleep in class again."

The crowd erupts with laughter and applauds at the conclusion of Carter's anecdote.

When the applause dies down Carter says, "And now ladies and gentlemen dinner is served. We will continue with speeches in about an hour followed by the dance. Enjoy."

At that instant waiters stream out of the kitchen carrying plates of food and serve everyone at the ball, starting with the head table.

Once everyone in the room finishes eating, their plates are cleared away and their drinks are freshened up. A few minutes later, Carter gets up and introduces the first of the ten guests seated at the head table. One by one, each of the guests at the head table get up and read their speeches, praising Admiral Stone, sharing short, funny anecdotes about him, congratulating him on a brilliant military career, and wishing him success in the future.

When everyone at the head table has finished giving their speeches Carter gets up and says, "And now it's time to hear from the guest of honor and my best friend, Admiral Nathan Stone."

As the admiral stands up, everyone in the room stands and applauds. He walks over to the podium, shakes Carter's hand and hugs him, and then Carter returns to his seat. After a couple of minutes, the applause dies down, and the admiral begins his speech.

"Thank you all for coming tonight. I am honored to have so many friends and colleagues here to wish me well in my retirement and it's good to see you all. For the past twenty-five years it has been my privilege and honor to help protect the people of Earth and Earth's sector of space."

"I started out as a fighter pilot and rose to command the most powerful warship ever built by man. I have seen many amazing things, some really weird things, and some truly frightening things in my travels. Memories of an amazing career I will carry with me always."

"Along with those memories there are some memories I wish I could truly purge from my mind. Like the time I walked in on my best friend Carter here, having zero gravity sex with a Rigellian female. At least I think it was female, it's kind of hard to tell because Rigellians look like a big featureless blob of purple Jell-O and I could never tell them apart."

The crowd erupts in a fit of laughter, the admiral looks down at his friend Carter who is laughing almost uncontrollably and proclaiming repeatedly, "It was definitely a female, it was definitely a female."

When the laughing dies down the admiral continues, "Seeing those two floating there was just wrong, and you can see why I would want to wipe that image from my mind."

There is another short burst of laughter and again the admiral continues, "Although I am retiring from the military, I am not actually retiring. As many of you know I am joining the Planetary Police Force so I will continue to serve Earth, but I will wear a different uniform."

"Carter and I will head up a new task force that will deal with criminal activity perpetrated by aliens and off-worlders anywhere in Earth's space. Our task force will work closely with the military to enforce our laws and protect our citizens."

"In closing, I would like to say that I am truly touched that you all wanted to be here tonight to wish me well and I want to thank you all for coming. Have a great time tonight, everyone."

The crowd gives the admiral a long, standing ovation, he waves to them and then takes his seat.

As the applause dies down, Carter stands up, takes the podium and announces, "Ladies and gentlemen the bars are open, and the dance will begin shortly."

Music starts playing and most of the people in the room stand and mingle, dance and line up at the bars to refresh their drinks.

A waiter comes by the head table with two tumblers full of scotch and offers them to Carter and Admiral Stone. They take the scotch and make their way around the room to mingle with the guests. Carter and the admiral visit with many old friends that they served with in their careers.

While speaking with a mutual old friend from their special forces days, the admiral notices a woman over Carter's left shoulder. She is a beautiful, petite, thin woman with long legs for her size. She has long, vibrant, auburn hair and is wearing a beautiful, emerald green, cocktail dress that sparkles when the lights hit it. She is sipping on a martini and every time the admiral looks at her, she is looking at him, but then she quickly looks away.

For the next hour, as the admiral moves around the room, the woman in green seems to follow him, but always keeps her distance, watching him just as before. The admiral's curiosity gets the best of him and he decides to approach her. He wants to surprise her, so he circles part way around the room and approaches her from the other side. As he walks up behind her, she is obviously looking around trying to see where he went.

The admiral leans in and whispers in her right ear, "He's not over there anymore."

The woman pauses for a moment and then slowly turns around to face him.

The first thought that runs through his mind is that she is even more beautiful up close and that she has very large, exquisite, brown eyes.

He realizes that he better say something, so he offers her his right hand and says, "Admiral Nathan Stone."

She takes his hand and says, "Nice to meet you, Admiral."

To which he replies, "And you are?"

She tilts her head to the right just a little and replies with a slightly devious smile on her face says, "An admirer of yours, Admiral."

He gives her a puzzled look for a second and then asks her, "Would you care to dance?"

She doesn't say a word she just offers him her hand, so he takes it in his hand and leads her out onto the dance floor. They spend the next hour dancing and talking, but she continues to be a little evasive about her identity.

Suddenly she turns towards him with a panicked look on her face and asks, "Quickly, what time is it?"

The admiral looks at his watch and says, "It's almost 23:00 hours."

The mysterious woman says, "Damn I have to go. Goodnight, Admiral."

Before he can stop her or say anything she vanishes into the crowd of guests. Puzzled, he wonders if he will ever see her again as he didn't get her name or her number.

The admiral goes back to find his friend Carter who is still drinking scotch and mingling with the guests. The admiral joins in on the fun, but his mind keeps wandering back to the mysterious woman in the green dress.

Several hours and many scotches later, the party is winding down. The admiral decides to head back to his hotel for the night. He says goodnight to Carter and several of the guests then makes his way outside, in front of the grand ballroom.

While waiting for the limousine to arrive, the beautiful, tall, blonde event coordinator, in the revealing, little, black dress, walks up beside him and links her arm around Nathan's. She smiles at Nathan and bats her big blue eyes at him.

"Heading back to your hotel, Admiral?"

"Yes, the limousine will be here shortly."

She smiles and then leans in close to whisper in his ear, "Would you like some company?"

He smiles back at her and says, "Yes, yes I would."

Just then the limousine pulls up, and the driver jumps out to open the door for his passengers.

Nathan holds, Heather's right hand while she gets into the car. Once seated, she slides across to the other side of the car so Nathan can get in and sit down.

The driver closes the door, walks around to the other side of the car, gets in, and they drive off, heading for the hotel.

Nathan opens the bar and asks, "Would you like some champagne, Heather?"

"I would love some, Admiral."

"Please, call me Nathan."

"Very well, Nathan."

Nathan pops the cork and pours two glasses of champagne. He hands one to Heather and takes the other for himself.

They clink their glasses together and Heather says, "Here's to your retirement and to a night that neither one of us will ever forget," then they both take a sip of champagne.

Heather puts her champagne glass down and then leans over and kisses Nathan aggressively, nibbling his lip just before breaking the kiss. She kisses him again and slides her hand down Nathan's body, stopping when she finds his growing erection.

She breaks the kiss, gives his erection a squeeze, and with a huge smile on her face says, "Oh my, I'm going to enjoy this."

She slides down off the seat, kneels on the floor and reaches for Nathan's zipper.

Nathan hits the button to raise the privacy shield so the driver can't see what they're doing.

Heather tugs his zipper down and pulls his large erection out of his pants. She wraps both hands around it and engulfs the rest in her mouth.

Nathan drops his head back on the seat and inhales sharply. Her warm mouth feels amazing.

Heather tries to take as much of his erection in her mouth as she can, but Nathan is fairly large so she can only get about half of it in.

It's a short drive from fleet headquarters to the hotel, so before long they are pulling into the hotel's driveway.

Heather quickly puts Nathan's erection back in his pants, zips them back up and gets back up on the seat.

The car stops, the driver gets out, comes around, and opens the door for his passengers.

Nathan steps out first and offers his hand to Heather to assist her in getting out of the car. After she steps out, Nathan hands the driver a fifty dollar bill and thanks him.

Nathan takes Heather's hand, leads her into the hotel lobby and over to the elevators. They step into a waiting elevator and Nathan pushes the button for the penthouse.

As soon as the doors close, Heather wraps her arms around Nathan and kisses him in an animalistic frenzy and grinds her pelvis against his erection.

Nathan knows he is in for a wild night.

Upon reaching his suite, Nathan opens the door for Heather, and as she walks in, she reaches back and unzips her little black dress. It falls to the floor, leaving her in just a pair of see through, black, lace panties, a matching shelf bra and a pair of black, stiletto high heels. She twirls around to show Nathan her sexy lingerie and her incredible body.

Nathan can tell Heather works out a lot as she is thin, toned and has the most amazing, perfectly round backside he has ever seen. He also guesses she knows a talented plastic surgeon, as her large, perfect breasts seem to defy gravity.

Heather walks towards the couch in the living room, swaying her hips almost hypnotically as she goes. When she reaches the couch, she turns and sits down, leans back into the corner and brings one leg up onto the couch.

Nathan walks towards her while undressing. He steps out of his dress shoes, drops his tuxedo jacket on the floor, undoes his bowtie, unbuttons his shirt, takes it off, and drops it on the floor.

Heather's eyes light up as she marvels at Nathan's muscular build. He is very fit with very little body fat so she can see every muscle clearly.

When Nathan reaches the couch, Heather sits up and undoes his pants, dropping them to the floor, followed by his underwear.

Nathan's large erection springs out of his underwear, right in front of Heather's face. She takes hold of it with one hand and marvels at its size. Heather takes him in her mouth and pleasures him once again.

Nathan inhales sharply and drops his head back, enjoying how her warm mouth feels.

After a few minutes, Nathan pushes Heather back into the couch and says, "My turn."

He straddles her on the couch, lowers his head, takes one of her nipples in his mouth, teases it with his tongue and then sucks and nibbles on it.

Heather drops her head back and moans softly, loving what Nathan is doing.

Nathan switches back and forth between her breasts, giving both of them a lot of attention. After a few minutes, Nathan kisses his way down her stomach to her little black panties.

Heather spreads her legs to give him access to what he craves.

Nathan kisses her through her panties a few times and then pulls her panties to the side. He notices that she is completely shaved save for a thin vertical line of hair.

Nathan looks up at her smiling face and says, "Oh my God, that is so sexy."

Nathan gently touches her with his tongue, causing Heather to close her eyes, arch her back, gasp and moan. She puts her hands in Nathan's hair as he continues to pleasure her.

She loves what Nathan is doing, and she knows it will not take long until she has her first orgasm of the night. Her pelvis thrusts towards his mouth, her breathing is rapid, and she is moaning like crazy.

Nathan captures her most sensitive spot with his lips and flicks it quickly with his tongue.

This immediately sends Heather over the edge, her body spasming as she is overtaken by an intense orgasm. Her hands tighten in his hair, her pelvis thrusts harder into his mouth, she is moaning and babbling incoherently, and her head is turning from side to side.

Nathan gives her a moment to recover before crawling up her body and spreading her legs wide. He pulls her panties to the side and positions his erection at her entrance. He lowers his head and kisses her gently as he thrusts his hips forward, entering her slowly and steadily.

Heather moans into Nathan's mouth as he slides inside her. When he is about half way inside her, he pulls back a little and thrusts forward again. Heather's moaning and their kissing intensifies as Nathan continues to thrust forward, going deeper and deeper.

After a few minutes, Nathan's pelvis touches hers which throws Heather into another intense orgasm. This time Nathan doesn't give her any time to recover. He pulls back slowly until he is just inside her, and then thrusts slowly all the way back in.

Heather throws her head back and arches her back as Nathan thrusts in and out of her. There is a mixture of moans, screams and incoherent words coming out of her mouth. The pleasure center of her brain is clearly overwhelmed by what Nathan is doing to her.

Nathan slowly increases the speed and force of his thrusting and Heather responds by thrusting her pelvis back up at him and moaning louder.

Nathan is surprised when Heather says, "H-h-h-harder... f-f-f-faster."

Nathan increases his pace and the force of his thrusts.

Again, she says, "H-h-h-harder... f-f-f-faster."

Nathan is now pounding into her as hard and as fast as he can.

Heather has gone back to babbling incoherently and is rapidly approaching another orgasm.

When it hits, she screams loudly and then yells, "OH GOD, DON'T STOP!"

Nathan continues thrusting into her as hard and as fast as he can.

Heather is writhing and screaming below him and seems to be in one long, continuous orgasm.

Nathan can feel his orgasm building quickly, and with one final thrust, buries himself deep as he explodes inside her, his body spasming almost uncontrollably. He collapses on top of her, both of them are panting like they've run a marathon.

While panting, Heather says, "Oh... my... God... that... was... amazing."

Nathan kisses her and says, "Oh... my... God... it... sure... was..."

The night is far from over for Nathan and Heather. Heather seems to be insatiable. She gets on all fours and has Nathan take her from behind on the couch.

After that, they jump in the shower and she has him pick her up and take her with her back against the glass wall of the shower. After the shower, she discovers there is a hot tub on the terrace.

She says, "I've never had sex in a hot tub before."

Nathan says, "Well then, tonight's the night."

Nathan turns on the hot tub, they open a bottle of champagne and climb in when it's warm enough.

Before Nathan knows it, Heather is straddling his lap and pressing her amazing, large breasts into his face. She lowers herself down onto his erection until he is deep inside her and then she rides him.

Nathan enjoys watching, playing with, and sucking on her breasts as she bounces up and down on his lap.

After the hot tub, they finally head over to the bed. Nathan is exhausted and thinks he can finally rest and get some sleep.

He thought wrong.

As soon as they get under the sheets, Heather turns and kisses him deeply, then reaches down, takes his manhood in her hand, and starts stroking it.

Nathan says, "Heather, I'm worn out."

She just giggles, dives under the sheets and takes him in her mouth again. Before long, her magical mouth has him fully erect and Heather is begging him to get on top of her and take her hard rough and fast.

Not able to resist this beautiful, sexy woman begging him to take her, he does just that. He climbs on top of her, spreads her legs wide and rams himself deep inside her in one hard thrust. She screams out in pleasure from being filled so full so quickly.

He immediately starts pounding into her as hard and as fast as he can. He is ravaging her like an animal, so it doesn't take long for her to reach orgasm. She is moaning and screaming as the waves of pleasure overtake her.

Nathan doesn't let up, and her body reacts by staying in orgasm. For the second time tonight, she is experiencing one long, continuous orgasm with no end in sight. Just like before, she is writhing, screaming, moaning, and babbling incoherently as Nathan ravages her.

A few minutes later, Nathan can feel his orgasm building, his body drenched in sweat from this frenzied session. With one final thrust, Nathan explodes inside her.

He looks down to see that, at some point, Heather passed out from the continuous, intense pleasure she was experiencing.

Nathan thinks to himself, "Oh thank God."

He looks at the clock and sees it's 03:11 hours, collapses beside her, rolls over and goes to sleep.

CHAPTER 3 - BACK HOME

The next morning, Nathan wakes with the sunrise, as the sun shines into his hotel suite and right in his face. He was so exhausted from having sex with Heather, he neglected to close the drapes last night before falling asleep.

Nathan rolls over to check on Heather and discovers he is alone in the bed. He looks around the room and sees there is no sign of her. She must have woken up at some point early this morning and let herself out.

Nathan looks at the clock and sees that it's now 05:06 hours and says, "Oh, it's way too early to be awake."

A few seconds later he says, "Wow, I never thought I would hear myself say that."

Being in the military for his entire adult life he was always out of bed and moving at 05:00 hours. Then the fact that he is no longer in the military, no longer an admiral, starts to sink in. For years now, he has introduced himself as Admiral Nathan Stone. Now that he has retired, he is just plain old Nathan Stone, something that will take him quite a while to get used to.

Still exhausted, he tells his brain to shut up, and then rolls over and goes back to sleep.

The next time he wakes it's 12:00 hours and since he has a flight to catch at 14:00 hours, he decides he better get out of bed and get moving. He gets up, showers, packs his things and then heads down to the lobby. He checks out of the hotel and then catches a cab to the airport.

When Nathan arrives at the airport, he heads over to the small business hangers. For this trip he has chartered a helijet to take him from Seattle to his home just outside of Jasper, Alberta in the Canadian Rocky Mountains.

He enters the hanger and is greeted by the owner of the company, who is also his pilot today. They hop in a bright yellow helijet, the pilot starts the engines, the rotors start to spin, he pushes the throttles up and soon they are lifting off the ground.

Once they reach about a thousand feet, the pilot pushes a second set of throttles up, the jet engines in the rear of the craft ignite, they accelerate rapidly, and soon Seattle is completely out of sight.

Later that afternoon they are flying through a beautiful, lush valley in the mountains, approaching Nathan's house in Jasper. The pilot lands the helijet on the large helipad next to Nathan's house. Nathan thanks the pilot, grabs his bag, and jumps out.

As he is walking towards the house, he says to himself, "It's good to be home."

He pauses at the door to watch the helijet take off, go straight up about two hundred feet and then zoom away at high speed. The helijet was out of sight in a matter of seconds.

Nathan unlocks the door, enters the house, and spends the next hour walking around the house checking to make sure everything is okay, removing the dust covers off all the furniture, and opening all the windows to let some fresh air in.

He decides he had better run into town and pick up some groceries, so he grabs the keys to his favorite classic muscle car, a 1969 Camaro Z28 painted in Daytona yellow with black stripes. He owns over a dozen classic muscle cars, trucks, and hotrods, but he drives the Z28 the most.

When he pulls into town with it, many people stop and stare because it's such a beautiful old car and because it makes a lot more noise than the today's electric cars.

When Nathan gets back from town, he unloads his groceries and makes himself dinner. After he has eaten and cleaned up, he pours himself a large tumbler of twenty-one-year-old single malt scotch, goes into the theater room, puts on a classic science fiction movie, and then settles into one of the reclining movie theater chairs to watch it. He only makes it through about half of the movie before falling fast asleep in the chair.

The next morning, he wakes up, looks at his watch, and sees that it's 09:00 hours. He gets up, makes himself breakfast and a coffee, then heads upstairs to have a shower. When he finishes his shower, he gets dressed in some work clothes and heads out to the large hangar behind the house.

Nathan opens the large main hangar door, walks inside, and looks up at a rather large ship. Then he looks to his right and sees about forty large wooden crates stacked neatly against the wall.

"I see everything was delivered as promised."

Nathan walks up the ramp into the lower bay of the ship and makes his way up to the bridge. He sits down in the helmsman's seat and looks around at the outdated controls.

"Oh man, I have a lot of work to do."

Just then he sees two police cruisers pull up and stop in front of the open hangar door. Carter gets out of the first cruiser and walks into the hangar.

Nathan makes his way down to the lower bay of the ship and then walks down the ramp into the hangar. Nathan and Carter meet halfway across the hanger floor, shake hands, hug, slap each other on the back, and then turn and look up at the ship.

They stand there examining the front of the ship and then Carter asks, "So this is it, huh?"

"Yup, I know she doesn't look like much now, but she will be amazing when I'm done with her."

Nathan points over at the forty large wooden crates and says, "When I get everything in those crates installed, she will be fast, have all the latest tracking gear, a cloaking device, holo-projectors, the latest in defensive shield technology, and she will be armed to the teeth."

Carter says, "I have a surprise for you that will make refitting the ship a lot easier."

"Oh, what's that?"

Carter turns to look at the police cruisers and gives a little wave.

All four doors on the second police cruiser open and four people get out, people that Nathan immediately recognizes.

Carter says, "They all approached me the other night at your retirement ball and asked me if they could join the Planetary Police Force to work with you. They all have the greatest respect for you and your command style, and they want to keep working with you. I went through their service records and determined they are all outstanding individuals who would make a great team. I've been working with the military to expedite their paperwork."

Nathan is dumbfounded from what he is seeing and hearing. These four people that served under him on the Invincible, respected him enough to change the course of their lives to continue working with him.

All four of these people had very important roles on the Invincible, Hiro Hashi Nagata (Japanese) was the chief engineer, James Bell (Canadian) was the helmsman and one hell of a pilot, Aleena Norata (Italian) was the tactical officer, and David Black (American) was the Marine captain, a medic and a weapons specialist.

All Nathan can think of to say is, "I don't know what to say."

Then the passenger door on Carter's police cruiser opens, and another woman gets out. Nathan recognizes her as the auburn-haired beauty he was dancing with at his retirement ball two nights ago. He quickly shoots Carter a puzzled look and sees that Carter has a smirk on his face and is trying not to laugh.

Carter says, "Her name is Desiree Arnoult, and she has been a police officer for five years now. She has an outstanding record and as soon as she heard that you were joining the force, she was in my office requesting to be made part of your team. She practically begged me to take her to your retirement ball. She wanted to meet you in the worst way, buddy."

Nathan looks at Carter and says, "You could have given me a heads up at the ball you know. What kind of friend are you, anyway?"

Carter slaps him on the back and replies almost chuckling, "I'm the best kind of friend, and what would be the fun in that?"

Nathan smiles, shakes his head and says, "I'll get you for that."

Carter waves for them to come over so the five of them walk over to the front of the ship to join Carter and Nathan.

Nathan greets the four former members of his crew, he shakes their hands and says, "I'm honored that you all went to such lengths because you wanted to continue serving with me, thank you."

He then turns to greet the mysterious woman. He smiles at her coyly, shakes her hand and says, "It's nice to meet you, Ms. Arnoult."

She smiles back at him and says, "Please, call me Desiree, Admiral."

"All right, Desiree, please call me Nathan."

Nathan takes a few steps back and says, "That goes for all of you, remember I am no longer an admiral and we are no longer in the military so please call me Nathan."

His eyes scan across the five new members of his team and he says, "I'm looking forward to getting to know you all a lot better", lingering a little too long when his eyes met Desiree's, both of them breaking the stare after a few awkward seconds.

Nathan turns and gestures towards the ship and says, "Let me introduce you to your new ship. She doesn't look like much now, but after we get everything in those crates installed and clean her up, she will be beautiful, fast and have some teeth."

He goes on to say, "Some of you may remember that we found this ship adrift in deep space about five years ago. I took her aboard the Invincible and brought her back to Earth as salvage. When I got her here, I tucked her away for a while. Now it's time to get her flying again."

They all wander around the ship, checking her out for a few minutes and then Nathan says, "Let's take you all into the house and get you settled in your rooms, have some lunch, and then we can come back out and get to work."

The five of them grab their bags out of the trunks of the two police cruisers and they head into the house.

As they enter the kitchen Carter asks, "Is there any beer in the refrigerator?"

Nathan turns and gives him a bit of a puzzled look and says, "What kind of question is that? Of course, there's beer in the fridge, I am Canadian after all."

Nathan's home is quite large and has more than enough space for everyone. One by one he shows them to their rooms. Desiree is the last to be guided to her room, and of course Nathan being a gentleman, carries her suitcase for her. He puts her suitcase down beside the bed and turns around to face her.

When their eyes meet, Desiree has this look on her face that is a dead giveaway. She is attracted to Nathan, and she's not being very subtle about it. Nathan wonders if she can tell that he is attracted to her as well.

He decides to play it cool and says, "Next to my room, this is the nicest room in the house, and it has a large bathroom with a nice big tub. Let me know if you need anything and we can drive into Jasper to pick up a few things."

Desiree doesn't say a word, she just keeps looking at him with a smile on her face like she is enjoying watching him try to be cool, seeing right through him.

Nathan starts to feel a little awkward and asks, "Shall we head back to the kitchen for lunch?", and then directs her out the door with his right hand.

Everyone assembles back in the kitchen after getting settled in their rooms. When Nathan and Desiree walk into the kitchen, Carter is leaning on the counter with his arms crossed. Nathan looks at Carter as he walks into the kitchen. Carter's eyes go back and forth between Nathan and Desiree and he smiles. He knows Nathan very well and he can see the attraction between them. Nathan smiles back, looks at the floor, and shakes his head slightly, acknowledging Carter's suspicion.

Nathan says to everyone, "There is plenty of food in the pantry, the fridge, and the freezer, so please help yourself. My home is now your home."

CHAPTER 4 - THE WORK BEGINS

The group has lunch together and then they head back out to the hangar.

Nathan says, "I think the first order of business should be to inventory everything in these crates to make sure everything we need is here."

So, they set about checking the shipping manifests and opening the crates to verify their contents. Afterwards, they present the manifests to Mr. Nagata so he can plan the installations and modifications.

The list of equipment is impressive including:

- a cloaking device
- the latest FTL star drive
- holographic projectors
- retractable laser turrets
- high yield particle beam weapons
- six-barrel Gatling style laser cannons
- retractable missile turrets
- wing mounted missile launchers
- nano-weapons emitters
- nano-missiles
- a new computer core and control system
- inductive / reflective shield generators.

Mr. Nagata says, "This is quite an impressive list of equipment and weapons. How did you manage to get a hold of such advanced military technology for a police cruiser?"

Nathan puts his hand on Mr. Nagata's shoulder and says, "One benefit of being a senior admiral in the EDF is the connections you make."

"Yes, of course. That was a silly question."

"We have six months to refit this ship with all this equipment. Think you can do it?"

After a slight pause Mr. Nagata says, "Six months? No problem."

Just then, from outside the hangar, the crew hears the high-pitched whine of multiple jet engines, coming closer, getting louder by the second.

Nathan says, "Oh, by the way, you can't use any space in either the rear hangar or the lower bay on the ship."

With a puzzled look on his face, Mr. Nagata asks, "Why?"

Nathan walks outside, points up to the sky and says, "We need the room for those."

The rest of the crew jogs out of the hangar and looks up just in time to see an F-114 Tomcat exo-fighter and a military six-person shuttle clear the treetops and come in for vertical landings on the helipad.

Immediately after the engines on the two craft shut down, the crew hears a diesel engine coming up the driveway. Soon a large truck and trailer comes around the corner into view. On the trailer is a large, military, six-wheel, all-terrain, troop transport with a menacing looking gun turret on top.

Nathan points and says, "We also need room for that."

A few minutes later several armored military transport trucks pull in behind the first truck and trailer.

Everyone looks at Nathan waiting to hear what's in those trucks, but Nathan just shrugs his shoulders and gives them his "your guess is as good as mine" look.

The driver from the lead truck gets out and walks over to Nathan. The driver recognizes the former admiral, so he snaps to attention and salutes him.

Nathan returns the driver's salute and says, "At ease, soldier."

The driver relaxes and presents Nathan with a tablet that contains the shipping manifest.

Nathan takes the tablet and scrolls through the manifest.

"Ahhhh, these are our small arms and amunit...," cutting off in mid-sentence.

Nathan looks at the driver in disbelief and asks, "Is this correct, soldier?"

The driver takes the tablet back and scans the manifest.

He hands the tablet back to Nathan and says, "Yes sir, that is correct."

Nathan looks at his crew who are anxiously waiting to hear what has Nathan so excited.

"They shipped us two of the fourth-generation armored exo-suits with special weapons packs and shields."

Mr. Black, being an ex-marine and the weapon specialist says, "Those suits haven't even been issued to the military yet, so how did we get two of them?"

Nathan flips through a few more pages of the manifest.

"Looks like they are a surprise from the Secretary of the Fleet, Admiral Hollister."

Mr. Black says, "I guess it's good to have friends in high places."

"Yes, it sure is, Mr. Black."

"All right everyone, let's get these trucks unloaded."

"Mr. Black, would you organize and secure the small arms in the weapons vault in the hangar for now?"

"Yes sir."

"Thank you, Mr. Black."

Once all the small arms are unloaded, they unload the crates containing the exo-suits and place them at the back of the hangar, so they are out of the way while they are working on the ship.

When all the trucks are unloaded, the drivers have Nathan sign the manifest saying he has received all the arms. They salute the former admiral and then they get in their trucks and drive off down the driveway. They are followed soon after by the large truck and trailer that dropped off the large, military, six-wheel, all-terrain, troop transport.

By the time all the small arms are organized and stored safely in the weapons vault, it's time for dinner.

Nathan says, "It's been a hell of a first day, so let's pack it in, go have a few cold frosty ones, and barbecue up some steaks for dinner."

They secure the hangar and head into the house to get cleaned up for dinner. After everyone has cleaned up, they meet back in the kitchen.

Nathan notices that Desiree has changed into some black stretch pants and a tight t-shirt that really shows off her curves.

His eyes linger a little too long on Desiree's ample breasts. When he looks up, Desiree is looking him right in the eyes and has a coy little smile on her face. Nathan knows she caught him. He feels his cheeks get warm as his face turns red.

To deflect he says, "Okay everyone, beers out on the deck before dinner."

Everyone grabs a beer out of the fridge, and then makes their way out onto the huge, multi-level deck on the back of the house. As they walk out on the deck, they can't help but stop and admire the beautiful Rocky Mountain view.

After a couple of beers, they all pitch in to make dinner. When everything is ready, they eat out on the deck while watching a beautiful sunset.

Once dinner and the dishes are done, it's about 21:00 hours.

Nathan asks, "So, what would you like to do now?"

Looking around all he gets in response are shoulder shrugs.

"Well I'm a 20th century movie buff, so how about we make some popcorn and watch an old science fiction movie?"

They all agree that sounds like a great idea and they head into the house to the home theater room.

Just before Nathan heads into the house, Desiree comes back out onto the deck. She walks up to him, wraps her arms around his right arm, looks up at him with those huge brown eyes and smiles.

"Nathan, would you mind if I sit beside you in case I need to ask a question about the movie?"

Nathan smiles and says, "Of course Desiree, it would be my pleasure."

"Great, thank you, Nathan."

She releases his arm and turns to walk back into the house. Nathan follows her towards the door, his eyes wandering down her body to admire her amazing backside as they walk.

Nathan's theater room has six, two-person recliner chairs in it and the floor is sloped down like a real movie theater so everyone can see the whole screen. Everyone takes a seat while Nathan makes a large batch of popcorn. When the popcorn is ready, he hands everyone a bowl of their own.

Nathan goes to sit down in the seat next to Desiree and the first thing he notices is her smile and the look of desire in her eyes. The second thing he notices is that she has folded the center armrest of the theater seats up so there will be nothing between them when he sits down.

Nathan smiles, sits down, and then reaches over and touches the glass-top table to the left of his chair. A holographic display appears, showing all the movie choices available in alphabetical order. Nathan spots one of his favorites and selects it to play.

"This is one of my favorite movies. It was made way back in 1979. It's a sci-fi horror called Alien. I think you'll like it."

They settle in to watch the movie. Nathan chuckles every time a scary part shocks everyone and makes them jump. He especially enjoys the reaction Desiree has to the scary parts of the movie, as every time she jumps, she grabs Nathan's right arm with both hands and holds on tight. Each time it happens they look at each other, chuckle a little, and then go back to watching the movie. The looks were lasting a little longer each time and Nathan notices how vibrant her smile is and how her eyes sparkle when she smiles.

After the movie finishes, the others get up, say goodnight and head to their rooms. Desiree stays to help Nathan clean up and then they walk together towards their rooms.

When they get to Desiree's door she smiles and says, "I really enjoyed that movie, I've never seen one from that time period before. Sorry that I kept grabbing your arm every time I got scared."

Nathan says, "I'm glad you enjoyed it and my arm is here for you to grab any time you get scared."

They stand there for a few seconds looking into each other's eyes, not saying a word. If anyone were watching, they would see the electricity flowing between them.

Finally, Nathan says, "We better get some sleep, we have a lot of work to do tomorrow."

"Yes, of course. Goodnight, Nathan."

"Goodnight, Desiree."

Desiree goes into her room and Nathan into his.

As Nathan turns to close his door, he catches a glimpse of Desiree sneaking one last peek for the night.

Knowing he caught her looking at him, Desiree quickly closes her door in embarrassment. Nathan closes his door and smiles.

Around 09:00 hours the next morning, the crew meets in the kitchen to make breakfast. Nathan cooks up some scrambled eggs, bacon and sausage. Mr. Bell is making pancakes, Mr. Black is making hash browns, and Mr. Nagata is making a large vat of coffee.

Desiree and Ms. Norata come in and sit down at the kitchen table to watch.

Desiree says, "Mmmm, I could get used to having the men make us breakfast every morning."

Ms. Norata high-fives her and says, "I heard that sister."

Nathan hears them giggling and turns to catch Desiree staring at him with a look of pure lust on her face. She doesn't change her expression after she realizes he's looking at her. Again, she's not being very subtle about it. She looks like she wants to throw him on the floor and ravage him. Her boldness has caught his attention, and it's arousing him.

After they finish breakfast and clean up, everyone heads out to the hangar to work on the ship. Mr. Nagata holds a small meeting under the nose of the ship to give the crew a basic game plan for the day. The first order of business is to remove all the old equipment to make room for the new. He splits the crew into teams of two and then assigns each team tasks for removing the old equipment. Mr. Nagata also lets them know that all harmful materials, such as the old reactor core, were removed years ago so they don't have to worry about any type of exposure.

After sending them off to work, he sits down at a work bench to work on the plan to fit all the new equipment into the allotted space in the ship. He has a lot of design work to do to fit all that new tech into the old ship. The ship is not small, but it sure seems to get smaller each time he adds another piece of new technology. Another challenge Mr. Nagata is facing is Nathan wants the exterior of the ship, as much as possible, to remain unchanged. He wants all the weaponry hidden. After all, this is a police cruiser, not a military assault ship.

The crew puts in a twelve-hour workday stripping the old technology out of the ship, but it seems as if they didn't even put a dent in it. They realize it will take a lot of work and a lot of long days to get this ship ready for active duty.

Everybody is pretty worn out, so they all head back to the house to get cleaned up for dinner. It's already getting late, so Nathan quickly barbecues up some hamburgers for dinner. After dinner and the dishes are finished, most of the crew settles into the comfy chairs in the theater room to watch another movie. Nathan grabs beers out of the fridge for everyone and then sits down in his seat to select a movie. Since everyone enjoyed Alien the night before, Nathan selects the sequel, Aliens, knowing that it's an even better science fiction movie than the original.

Just then Desiree wanders in and sits down beside Nathan, she had changed into a pair of sweats and a sweater to be comfortable.

The movie plays, Nathan sits back in his seat and turns his head to glance over at Desiree. Desiree catches this out of the corner of her eye and turns to look at Nathan. Their eyes meet and lock onto each other for a few seconds, they both smile and then turn back to watch the movie.

About half an hour into the movie, Desiree notices Nathan's right hand is hanging off a throw pillow. It's in perfect position for her to just slide her left hand under it, but she doesn't know if she should or not. She decides to go for it, so she slides her hand under his and takes hold of it. Nathan is pleasantly surprised and looks from their hands to Desiree's smiling face. He gives her hand a gentle squeeze and then goes back to watching the movie with a big smile on his face.

It was a long hard day of working on the ship, so Nathan is not surprised when, about halfway through the movie, he looks over at Desiree to find her fast asleep.

Nathan sits there looking at her, taking in how beautiful she is, and thinking how much he would like to kiss her at that moment.

Nathan lets go of her hand, gets up and goes over to a bin at the back of the theater room. He pulls out a soft fleece blanket, brings it over to her, and covers her up with it. He then sits back down to enjoy the rest of the movie.

When the movie ends, Nathan gets up, looks around, and realizes he is the only one still awake. Everyone else is sound asleep. After turning off all the equipment in the theater room, he retrieves more blankets and covers each of them up, thinking it's best just to leave everyone where they are. Everyone except Desiree that is. He scoops Desiree up in his arms, carries her to her room, and gently lays her down on her bed. He tucks the soft fleece blanket in around her and then just stands there looking at her beautiful face. Unable to resist temptation, he bends down and gently kisses her on the lips.

He whispers, "Goodnight, Desiree," then turns and walks out of the room closing the door behind him.

Desiree smiles and whispers, "Goodnight, Nathan," then rolls over and goes back to sleep.

In the morning Nathan and the other crew members are in the kitchen making breakfast when Desiree walks in.

She heads straight over to Nathan and wraps her arms around his right arm.

"Thanks for tucking me in last night, that was sweet of you."

"Oh, you're welcome, Desiree."

She stands on her tip toes, leans in and whispers in his ear, "And thank you for the goodnight kiss too."

She pulls back, smiles, gives Nathan a quick wink, and then sits down at the kitchen table. Nathan chuckles to himself, shakes his head a little, and continues making breakfast.

When everyone is done eating, they clean up and then head out to the hangar to work on the ship, continuing to strip the old technology out of her.

For the next four days, the crew follows the same routine of stripping old technology out of the ship and watching old science fiction movies at night to wind down.

The attraction between Desiree and Nathan continues to grow, as does the sexual tension. Each night Nathan walks her to her room and kisses her goodnight. Each night the kisses get longer and longer.

On several occasions, when changing before dinner, Desiree would leave her bedroom door open while she changed her clothes so when Nathan was going into his room he would "accidentally" see her in a sexy bra and panty set and she would pretend to be oblivious to him watching her.

One night when they were getting ready to watch a movie, Desiree came out of her room wearing a loose-fitting sweatshirt that had three buttons at the collar, and all three buttons were undone. Nathan was already seated in the theater room ready to watch the movie when Desiree came in.

Instead of sitting down beside him she walked up, placed her hands on the headrest and the arm of the chair, bent over at the waist and whispered seductively in his ear, "Is there anything you would like before we start the movie?"

She then pulled back a little so she could see his face, knowing full well her shirt has fallen wide open and he could see her beautiful breasts and the sexy, lime green, lace, push-up bra she put on specially for him.

The look on his face was one of shock and lust and he barely manages to squeak out, "I would love a scotch."

Desiree goes to the bar and pours him a tumbler full of twenty-one-year-old single malt scotch. She comes back, sits down beside Nathan in the theater seats and hands him the drink.

After a few seconds, she leans over as he is taking his first sip of scotch and whispers in his ear, "To answer the question that's in your mind right now, yes, the panties I'm wearing match my bra."

Hearing this causes Nathan to choke on his scotch and cough and sputter, which makes Desiree laugh.

Nathan could hardly concentrate on the movie because he couldn't get the image of Desiree in the sexy, little, lime green, bra and panties out of his mind.

The next night after dinner, Desiree tells everyone she is exhausted, that she's going to go relax in a nice hot tub, and then go to sleep.

Nathan is very disappointed, so he has trouble getting into the movie that night. He watches about forty minutes of the movie and then decides to go have a quick shower and go to sleep. After his shower he walks out into his bedroom and turns down his bed. Just then there is a quiet knock on his door, so he quickly throws on his bath robe and opens the door. What he sees causes him to freeze, his heart to pound, and his stomach to fill with butterflies.

Standing before him is Desiree, dressed in a sexy, semi-sheer, short, black, baby doll nightie. Underneath that, Nathan can see she is wearing tiny, black, lace, string bikini panties. Finishing off her sexy ensemble is a pair of black stiletto high heels. Her makeup and her hair are all done up, and she has a very seductive look on her face. Her large, perfect breasts are clearly visible through the nightie and have caught Nathan's attention.

Nathan stands there for a second or two drinking in her sexiness when she pushes him back into his room and closes the door behind them. They grab each other and kiss passionately, their hands exploring each other's bodies.

Nathan's hands come to rest on her breasts and he gently squeezes them which causes Desiree to moan softly.

Desiree's hands are busy opening Nathan's robe, which once open, slides off his shoulders onto the floor leaving Nathan naked in front of her.

Desiree takes a few seconds to admire Nathan's muscular, toned body and his large erect manhood before he picks her up, carries her over to the bed, and sets her down gently.

Desiree hooks her thumbs in the waistband of her tiny black panties and slides them seductively down her legs before tossing them across the room.

Nathan eagerly accepts her invitation and crawls onto the bed with her. Desiree spreads her legs as Nathan positions himself over her.

Their excitement causes them to rush and skip foreplay, Nathan enters her slowly and steadily until he is all the way inside her.

Desiree throws her head back and moans loudly as Nathan takes her.

Nathan lowers his head and captures her mouth with his, not just kissing her, but making love to her mouth with his. He teases her lips with his, barely touching as he moves his head from side to side, their tongues dancing with each other, then kissing her forcefully as he starts to make love to her.

The excitement is too much for Desiree, she moans into his mouth, her body overtaken by a very powerful orgasm that seems to go on forever. Her body convulsing uncontrollably with every thrust with no sign of stopping.

Seeing Desiree writhe beneath him, hearing her moans, and knowing she is experiencing one long continuous orgasm is too much for Nathan. It quickly pushes him over the edge, his pace quickens, and he explodes inside her, his body wracked in an intense orgasm.

When the two lovers come back to reality Nathan practically falls on the bed beside her, exhausted and panting like he just ran a marathon.

Desiree says, panting heavily, "OH... MY... GOD..., THAT WAS INCREDIBLE!"

Nathan can't even speak, he just smiles and nods his head.

The two make passionate love three more times before falling asleep, totally exhausted, wrapped in each other's arms.

The next morning the two lovers awaken still wrapped in each other's arms. They smile at each other and kiss.

Nathan says, "Good morning, sexy."

"Mmmm, good morning you sexy, sexy man."

Nathan looks at the clock, smiles and says, "Oh-oh, we missed breakfast."

They get dressed, grab something to eat and head out to the hangar.

When they get there, the other crew members all stop what they are doing and applaud.

Ms. Norata says, "It's about time."

Mr. Bell says, "We've been wondering when you two would finally get together."

Nathan and Desiree are a little embarrassed, but they smile and give each other a hug and a kiss in front of everyone.

When the hoopla dies down, Mr. Nagata calls a meeting to go over his plans to install all the new equipment. Everyone gathers around his work bench so they can see the blueprints he has drawn up, and he begins to layout the processes and timelines to install all the new technology in the ship. He lets everyone know that they have about five months of hard work ahead of them to get this ship ready for service. If they all work together as a team, they can get it done, and when finished, this ship will be the most advanced ship the police force has. She will be fast, tough and mean. He assigns tasks to the teams of two he assembled previously, and they all get to work.

CHAPTER 5 - THE JOB DOESN'T GO AS PLANNED

Just outside of Seattle Washington, an armored, military, high-speed, hover train is racing along the tracks, heading for the EDF's logistics yard just outside of Washington D. C. It left EDF headquarters in Seattle about forty-five minutes before, and it has been winding its way through the Rocky Mountains. After clearing the mountains, it starts a long straight run through Idaho and Montana, so the engineer increases speed to two hundred miles per hour as the tracks are a fair distance away from any populated areas.

The train cruises on the straightaway for just a few minutes, when a small spacecraft appears in the distance and quickly blasts in over top of the train. When the ship reaches the third train car, it matches the speed of the train and drops down to about fifteen feet above the car.

A large hatch opens on the bottom of the ship and four ropes drop out and land on the roof of the car. A few seconds later four men dressed in black fatigues and assault helmets slide down the ropes to the train. Each man has an assault rifle of some type slung over their backs. The second they land on the train, they draw their weapons and take a defensive stance, each man watching a different direction.

One man has an additional pack on his back. After a few seconds he is satisfied they are secure, so he slings his rifle and drops the pack on the roof of the train.

He kneels down, opens the pack and removes a mechanical device. He pulls open the tripod legs of the device and sets it in the middle of the roof. Once he has positioned it, he extends a mechanical arm out from it and clicks a button on the top of the device. The arm emits a beam from its tip and rotates, cutting a large hole in the car's roof.

Just before the device finishes cutting the hole, the man grabs the device and deactivates the beam as the piece of the roof falls into the car with a loud metallic clang. The man collapses the device and stuffs it back into the pack. He pulls out a small hand mirror and puts his hand into the hole so he can see what is in the car. All he sees is a small green crate sitting on the floor in the middle of the car, so he puts the mirror away, stands up and then drops into the hole.

As his feet hit the floor, the crate vanishes and six Marines, with their pulse rifles pointed at him, appear.

They yell, "FREEZE! DON'T MOVE! HANDS UP!"

He quickly assesses the situation and realizes he is caught, so he puts his hands up.

He yells into his radio, "IT'S A TRAP! BAIL! BAIL! BAIL!"

The three men on the roof of the train grab their lines and the ship veers off, banking to the right and climbing. The lines are drawn up into the ship, pulling the men back inside, the hatch closes, the ship accelerates, heads for space, and is soon out of sight. As soon as the ship breaks orbit, it accelerates away, enters FTL, and disappears in a bright blue flash of light.

Back inside the train, the Marines are disarming the man they apprehended and cuffing his hands behind his back. The Marine in charge of the squad radios that the prisoner is secure.

The train stops at the next small town where a police cruiser is waiting. The Marines hand the prisoner off to the police who take him aboard the cruiser and place him in a holding cell. The cruiser takes off, heads back to Seattle at high speed and lands at the Planetary Police headquarters a short time later.

When the cruiser touches down Carter is standing there waiting. The officers escort him down the ramp of the cruiser and past Carter into police headquarters.

He is taken into the prisoner processing area where he is scanned for identification, weapons and foreign objects. He is then given a standard orange prison jumpsuit with a number on it.   Once he has changed into the orange jumpsuit, he is escorted to an interview room, handcuffed to a loop in the middle of the table and then left alone in the room to sweat.

After watching him sweat through the cameras for about an hour, Carter enters the interview room, drops a tablet displaying the prisoner's file on the table, and sits down across from the prisoner.

Carter examines the file for a few seconds and says, "Marcus Haggerty. That is your name isn't it? You have quite the rap sheet here."

The prisoner looks back at him with no emotion showing on his face and he doesn't say a word.

"Well Mr. Haggerty, in case you were wondering how you were caught so easily, we knew you were coming. Your communications were being intercepted and decrypted. We knew everything about your plan, so we diverted the shipment you were after and setup the holo-projectors that made you think the train car was empty except for that one crate."

After hearing this, the expression on the prisoner's face gets a little more intense, but still he says nothing.

"We know that Captain Creeksto of the Sulari hired you to steal that crate. A crate full of some obscure ore from a tiny little planet in Earth's space called Trynx 3. It's only a matter of time before we catch up to Captain Creeksto and your crew, so why don't you help yourself?"

"If you help us find Captain Creeksto and your crew, we will cut you a deal. You'll serve minimal time here on Earth instead of being sent off to a penal asteroid for twenty years."

Still the prisoner says nothing, and his expression does not change.

"Do you know why Captain Creeksto wants this ore so badly?"

Still no reaction from the prisoner.

"You know a good friend of mine dealt with Creeksto a little while back. He was asking for passage through Earth's space to Trynx 3 but wouldn't give a reason why he wanted to go there. So, my friend refused him passage. Creeksto got aggressive. At that time, my friend was an admiral in the EDF whose motto was, 'walk softly and carry a giant aircraft carrier'. Needless to say, he sent Creeksto packing."

The prisoner says nothing, so Carter gets up and heads for the door.

"Let me know if you change your mind."

Carter exits the room and instructs the guards to take the prisoner to a holding cell.

The next day the prisoner is taken to a nearby courthouse to appear before a judge. The charges against him are read, and he is asked to enter a plea. The prisoner still refuses to say a word, so the judge sets his trial date and orders that he be held in a maximum-security prison nearby until his trial in six months.

The prisoner is taken by armored transport to the prison and escorted by six armed guards to his cell. On his way in he sees all manner of diabolical looking creatures in the cells of the prison block. When they reach his cell, he is escorted into his cell by one guard. The other five guards remain outside the cell, keeping their weapons trained on him. The one guard removes the prisoner's shackles and exits the cell, the door sliding closed behind him.

The prisoner looks around the small dark gray cell and then lies down on the bed. He puts his hands behind his head and closes his eyes to get some sleep, but sleep does not come easy. The noises in the prison combined with the thought of spending the next six months there keeps him awake for most of the night.

CHAPTER 6 - TEST FLIGHT

After five months of hard work, Nathan's team has finished refitting, rearming, and repainting their ship. Mr. Nagata has pulled off a miracle and met all of Nathan's criteria by fitting all the new technology in without too many changes to the exterior of the ship. He has hidden all the new weaponry behind the leading edge of the wings and a few retractable turrets on the fuselage. He fit the new reactor, computer core, shield generator, FTL drive, cloaking device, and holo-system in while still leaving plenty of room for living quarters. He also made sure that there was enough room in both bays for the fighter, the shuttle, and the six wheeled all-terrain troop transport. The bridge was stripped to the bulkheads and rebuilt with state-of-the-art technology. He went through the jet and sub-light engines, putting them back into perfect working order. He also repaired the diverter and vent system that allows the ship to perform vertical takeoffs and landings. All the remaining systems on the ship were torn apart, cleaned, repaired and reassembled.

The ship was then repainted in a nostalgic black and white paint scheme used by many police forces in the late twentieth century. Nathan provided the finishing touches by decaling the ship with the planetary police force badge and nostalgic slogans like "To Serve and Protect". He also added a series of red and blue flashing lights around the exterior of the ship including a large light bar mounted above the windows of the bridge. The old derelict ship has been fully transformed into the quintessential high-tech police cruiser with a classic look to it.

With all the major work done, the next steps are to check to make sure that all systems are working, do a hull pressure check, and take her up for a test flight and weapons checks.

For the first time in years, the ship is hooked up to a tug, pulled out of the hangar and over to the helipad.

The crew stands back to admire their handiwork. The ship looks beautiful sitting there shining in the bright sunlight with the amazing Rocky Mountains as a backdrop.

Nathan says, "Okay everyone, it's picture time."

The crew is all dressed in their uniforms and flight gear, so Nathan directs them where he wants them to stand then sets the camera up.

He joins his crew and says, "Okay everyone, smile."

Nathan pushes the button on the camera's remote control to take the picture. He checks the camera to make sure the picture was a good one and then packs up the camera.

"Okay, let's get on board for the pre-flight systems check and hull pressure test."

Mr. Nagata opens the ramp to the lower bay, the crew boards the ship and makes their way up to the newly redesigned high-tech bridge to start their pre-flight tests.

Nathan takes the captain's chair in the center of the bridge, Desiree takes a seat at the communications station, Mr. Bell takes the pilot's chair, Mr. Black takes the navigator's chair, Ms. Norata takes a seat at the tactical station and Mr. Nagata takes a seat at the engineering station.

Over the next two hours they go through all the major systems on the ship. It's no surprise that every system passes. Next, they close all the hatches, ports and vents on the ship to perform the hull pressure test. They pressurize the interior of the ship to three atmospheres and check every section for leaks using a handheld scanning device. After two hours of checking for leaks, Nathan declares the ship ready for its first atmospheric flight test. Everyone heads back up to the bridge, takes their stations, and begins their pre-launch sequence.

When everyone is ready Nathan says, "Mr. Bell, fire up the jet engines."

"Aye sir."

The jet engines emit a high-pitched whine as they wind up.

"Ms. Arnoult, contact Jasper air traffic control and request clearance for a vertical takeoff."

"Aye sir."

A few moments later Ms. Arnoult says, "Sir, Jasper air traffic control has granted us clearance for vertical takeoff, no traffic in the immediate area."

"Thank you, Ms. Arnoult."

"Mr. Bell?"

Mr. Bell turns around to look at Nathan and says, "Yes sir?"

"It's time. Let's take her up."

Mr. Bell smiles and says, "Aye sir."

He turns back around and begins the takeoff procedures.

On the outside of the ship the diverters lower and the vertical takeoff vents open, directing the thrust from the jet engines down towards the ground. Mr. Bell grabs the throttles with his right hand and slowly pushes them forward, increasing the power until the ship rises.

The crew on the bridge looks around at each other with big smiles on their faces, happy knowing that all their hard work has paid off, leading them to this moment, the maiden voyage of their new police cruiser.

As the ship ascends and clears the trees, the crew can see the beautiful valley they have been living in for the past six months. The majestic mountains and a lot of clear blue sky all around them.

When the ship reaches two hundred feet, Mr. Bell hits a button and the ship's systems adjust the diverters and vents to change from vertical takeoff to flight mode. The nose of the ship comes up slightly and the ship starts to move forward. Mr. Bell retracts the landing gear, then pushes the throttles about halfway open. The ship accelerates and climbs rapidly, pushing the crew back in their seats. When the ship reaches thirty thousand feet, Mr. Bell pulls back on the throttles a bit, slowing the ship down.

"Mr. Black, set course two seven zero degrees, due west over the Pacific Ocean."

"Aye sir, course laid in."

"Mr. Bell, change course and take her up to five hundred knots."

"Aye sir."

Mr. Bell turns the ship and pushes the throttles forward slightly.

A minute later Mr. Bell says, "Sir, our heading is now two seven zero degrees traveling at five hundred knots."

"Thank you, Mr. Bell."

About an hour and a half later, the ship clears the coastline and heads out over the Pacific Ocean.

Nathan says, "Okay, Mr. Bell, let's see what she's got."

"Aye sir."

Mr. Bell pushes the throttles wide open, and the ship accelerates rapidly. He calls out the air speed as it hits key levels.

"Mach one, mach two, mach three, mach four, mach five........."

He continues until the ship stops accelerating, at which point, he turns around to look at Nathan with a big smile on his face.

"Sir, we have reached our maximum velocity of mach eight point five."

The crew cheers and applauds, happy that their ship has passed the first flight test of the day.

"Mr. Bell, reduce speed to mach one point five."

"Aye sir."

He pulls back on the throttles and the ship decelerates.

Two minutes later Mr. Bell says, "Sir, we have slowed to mach one point five."

"Thank you, Mr. Bell."

"Ms. Arnoult, contact Earth space flight control and get clearance for space flight."

"Aye sir."

A minute later Desiree says, "Sir, Earth space flight control has granted us clearance for space flight, no traffic in the immediate area."

"Thank you, Ms. Arnoult."

"Mr. Bell, take her up."

"Aye sir."

Mr. Bell rams the throttles wide open, pushing the crew back in their seats. He pulls the nose of the ship up and heads for space. Several minutes later, the sky around the ship turns black and the stars appear as they near the edge of the planet's atmosphere. At this point Mr. Bell disengages the jet engines and closes the air intakes. He then engages the sub-light engines and rams the throttles wide open. The ship accelerates, almost violently, to achieve escape velocity.

The ship's computer announces in its female voice, "Now leaving Earth's gravity. Artificial gravity plating is coming online."

Nathan says, "Mr. Black, plot a course for the asteroid belt at the outer edge of the solar system."

"Aye sir, course laid in."

"Thank you, Mr. Black."

"Mr. Bell, engage the FTL drive and take us to the asteroid belt, speed 4 TSL."

"Aye sir, engaging the FTL drive now."

The ship accelerates rapidly, and the crew sees a bright blue flash of light through the bridge windows as the ship enters FTL.

A minute later Mr. Bell announces, "We have reached 4 TSL. It'll only take a few minutes to get to the asteroid belt."

"Thank you, Mr. Bell."

After a few minutes Mr. Bell says, "Sir, we are approaching the asteroid belt."

"Very well, Mr. Bell, drop us out of FTL."

"Aye sir, dropping us out of FTL now."

A few seconds later there is a bright blue flash of light through the bridge windows as the ship drops out of FTL. Through the bridge windows the crew sees thousands of asteroids in all shapes and sizes.

Nathan says, "Ms. Norata, bring the shields online, full power in reflective mode."

"Aye sir, shields up at full power in reflective mode."

"All right, Ms. Norata you may begin your weapons tests."

"Aye sir, tests will commence shortly, starting with the laser turrets."

"Very well, Ms. Norata, you may fire when ready."

"Aye sir, laser turrets deployed, target acquired.... firing."

From both sides of the ship's fuselage and underneath the ship, erupts a series of powerful red laser blasts. A split second later, a very large asteroid, floating about two kilometers in front of the ship, explodes with a brilliant flash.

Ms. Norata says, "Arming particle beam weapons, target acquired.... firing."

From the tips of the wings erupt two, long, red, sparkling beams. Just as with the laser turrets, another large asteroid explodes with a brilliant flash.

Ms. Norata says, "Arming the Gatling lasers, target acquired.... firing."

There are two Gatling lasers mounted in the leading edge of each wing. Each one can fire sixty laser bursts per second or thirty-six-hundred laser bursts per minute. With their rate of fire, Ms. Norata was able to cut a very large asteroid completely in half in less than two minutes.

As the two halves of the asteroid float away, Ms. Norata says, "Arming missiles, targets acquired.... firing."

Two missiles fire from the launchers mounted in the leading edge of wings and streak towards the two pieces of asteroid. The missiles obliterate the asteroid halves on contact.

Next on the list are the nano-emitters. Ms. Norata releases two man made targets from a small cargo hatch in the ship's nose. They seem to be glass and steel boxes with a metal sphere inside.

"Arming the nano-emitters, target acquired.... firing."

Nothing happens. No blast, no flash, nothing at all. The crew looks around at each other, wondering what went wrong. All except Nathan and Ms. Norata that is. They sit, arms crossed, patiently watching the view screen with a slight smile on their faces.

Suddenly, the glass on the two boxes cracks and blows out, leaving just the metal frame of the boxes, and the metal spheres in the center. The other crew members look around at each other, puzzled as to what just happened. Thirty seconds later the spheres explode, surprising the crew, and destroying the boxes completely.

Ms. Norata explains to the crew, "The nano-emitters released an invisible cloud of nanobots that penetrated the glass and the spheres and then set off the explosives inside.

The nano-emitters are used for close quarters and stealth situations."

Ms. Norata continues, "We also have these nanobots in a missile deployment system for targets that are farther away, which I will test right now."

She releases two more targets into space, but this time she waits until the targets are a little farther away before she arms and fires the weapons. The missiles fire from the launchers mounted in the leading edge of the ship's wings. They streak toward the targets and just before they impact, there is a large puff of smoke from each missile, and then the missile breaks up into hundreds of small pieces with no explosion.

The crew looks around at each other with a look on their faces like they are all thinking, "Was that supposed to happen?"

Then just like before the glass blows out of the targets and then shortly after the spheres explode.

Ms. Norata explains to the crew, "The nanobots are delivered in an invisible cloud after the missile casing disintegrates. The enemy will think the missiles were duds, at least until the nanobots start causing damage. To my knowledge no known species has technology capable of defending against these nanobots. They are so small they can pass right through a vessel's shields undetected."

Nathan stands up from his chair and says, "Well I guess there is only one last system to test. The shields, and there is only one way to test them."

Nathan walks off the bridge leaving his crew a little puzzled as to what he meant by that.

About five minutes later the ship's computer announces, "Rear shuttle bay doors opening."

Mr. Black says, "Is he going to do what I think he's going to do?"

Ms. Norata smiles and says, "Yes, yes he is. Switching shields to inductive mode. The fighter has left the bay."

A few seconds later they see the F-114 Tomcat fly past the front windows of the ship at VERY close range. Nathan takes the fighter out about five kilometers and then turns around one hundred and eighty degrees to start his run.

Over the comm system Nathan says, "I'm setting the weapons at ten percent power."

Ms. Norata says, "Aye sir, we're ready."

Nathan opens up with a barrage from the Gatling lasers mounted in the wings of the fighter.

Ms. Norata watches the shields on her console.

She smiles and says, "Shield power up to one hundred and ten percent, sir. The induction works perfectly. They absorbed every bit of energy and strengthened themselves."

Nathan says, "Excellent. Switch the shields to reflective mode. I'm gonna make another run."

"Aye sir, shields set to reflective mode."

Once again, Nathan takes the fighter out about five kilometers, turns around one hundred and eighty degrees and starts his run. He opens up with another barrage from the Gatling lasers, but this time the blasts are reflected away from the ship in all directions, including right back at Nathan. Nathan reacts by rolling the fighter to the right and diving.

Ms. Norata says, "Reflective mode worked perfectly sir, the shields reflected one hundred percent of the blasts and are stable at one hundred and five percent."

Nathan responds with, "Excellent. I'm bringing her in."

Nathan flies the fighter around to the back of the ship.

The fighter's computer voice comes on and says, "Automated landing systems engaged, please release all controls."

Nathan takes his hands and feet off the controls. The fighter slows down and aligns itself with the shuttle bay. The landing gear comes down, the fighter passes through the atmospheric force field and touches down right in the center of the shuttle bay. As soon as the fighter touches down, the fighter's computer powers down the engines and opens the canopy. At the same time, the ship's computer closes the shuttle bay doors.

Nathan pushes a button on the dash of the fighter. A series of steps and a small ladder unfold from the fuselage. Nathan removes his helmet, releases his harness, climbs out of the cockpit and down the ladder to the deck. Using a small robotic tug, he parks the fighter to the side of the bay. He then tethers it to the deck to keep it in place during flight. With the fighter secured, Nathan heads back up to the bridge, upon entering he takes his seat.

"Well I think today's tests were a complete success and the ship is ready for service."

The crew acknowledges, "Aye sir."

"Mr. Black, plot a course for home."

"Aye sir, course laid in."

"Thank you, Mr. Black."

"Mr. Bell, take us home. Speed 4 TSL."

"Aye sir, 4 TSL for home."

Mr. Bell swings the ship around and says, "Hold on to your butts."

The ship accelerates rapidly and soon the crew sees a bright blue flash of light through the bridge windows as the ship enters FTL.

Nathan chuckles and says, "Mr. Bell I thought you were asleep during that part of Jurassic Park. Hold on to your butts indeed. Next thing you know the button to engage the FTL drive will have a little sticker around it that says Go

Baby Go just like the nitrous oxide button the Eleanor Mustang had in Gone In 60 Seconds."

Mr. Bell turns around with a big smile on his face and says, "Too late."

"Are you kidding me?"

Nathan gets up and walks over to Mr. Bell's station to look. Sure enough, there is a sticker around the button to engage the FTL drive that says, "Go Baby Go."

Nathan chuckles, shakes his head and walks back to his chair. He sits there for a minute and then gets up and heads for the bridge door.

As he exits the bridge he says, "Take us back to Jasper, standard approach and landing procedures. I'll be in my cabin."

The crew answers, "Aye sir."

Nathan heads back to his cabin to retrieve a box and before too long he sees a bright blue flash of light through his window as the ship drops out of FTL. He walks over to his window and looks down on Earth as the ship enters the atmosphere. Soon the jet engines kick in and within about fifteen minutes they are landing in Jasper on his helipad.

Nathan grabs the box and slides the top open revealing a nice bottle of champagne. He takes the bottle out and heads down the hall to the galley where he grabs six champagne flutes. After that he heads back up to the bridge. When he enters the bridge, everyone is just getting up from their seats after shutting all the ship's systems down. Nathan sets the glasses down on one of the consoles.

"It's time to celebrate the successful maiden flight and systems tests. The ship performed beautifully, and her crew did an excellent job."

Nathan pops the top on the champagne, fills the glasses, and hands one to every member of the crew.

"A toast, to rebirth and to the finest crew on the force."

They all clang their glasses together and drink the champagne.

Nathan says, "Okay everybody out. It's dinner time and I'm hungry. Let's head into the house and make dinner."

Everyone heads down to the lower bay of the ship. Nathan lowers the ramp, everyone exits the ship and then Nathan closes the ramp behind him. They go into the house and make their way into kitchen to grab beers out of the fridge. They all help to make dinner and spend the night eating, drinking, listening to music on the deck, and enjoying a warm summer night in the mountains.

CHAPTER 7 - TRIAL AND SENTENCING

After six months of sitting in his cell in a maximum-security prison, Marcus Haggerty is being taken back to the courthouse for trial. Six prison guards are assigned to move him to the armored transport waiting outside. They open his cell door, one guard enters the cell to put the shackles on him, while the other five guards stand outside his cell with their weapons pointed at him. Once he is shackled, the guards escort him to an armored transport truck waiting in a high security loading bay. They secure him in a cage in the rear compartment of the truck.

The transport truck leaves for the courthouse with two armed guards in the cab and two more in the rear compartment with Haggerty. As the transport truck exits the prison, through no less than three security gate checkpoints, it's joined by two police cruisers, an armored troop transport with a laser cannon turret on top, and a police helijet flying over-watch.

When the motorcade arrives at the courthouse, it drives down a long ramp and enters a secure underground level. Haggerty is unloaded from the back of the truck and the armed guards escort him into the building to a high-tech holding cell. The guards sit him down on the bench in the cell, and then they back out and activate the force field.

Haggerty looks around the cell sizing up the security systems and quickly realizes that any attempt to escape would be foolish. His every move is being watched by four cameras and several sensor arrays. In addition, there are several systems in place including knockout gas, tasers and restraining gel to incapacitate him should he try anything.

He doesn't have to wait for long before a couple of rather large court bailiffs come and deactivate the cell's force field. After entering the cell, they each take hold of an arm, pick him up and walk him, still shackled, into the court room. In the court room, one bailiff orders him to take a seat at the table reserved for the defendants. Sitting beside him at the table is his court appointed defense council. The lawyer doesn't even bother to introduce himself.

He leans over and whispers, "You were caught red handed so how about we just save ourselves some time and plead you guilty?"

Haggerty just looks at him with a blank look on his face and doesn't say a word. He shows no reaction of any kind.

Just then the judge enters from his chambers behind the bench.

One bailiff yells, "ALL RISE! THE HONORABLE J. P. MONROE PRESIDING!"

Everyone, except Haggerty, stands up. The judge notices but says nothing.

The judge sits down and says, "You may be seated."

The judge puts on his reading glasses and takes a few minutes to read through the case file and the police report. When he has finished going over the case, he tilts his head and looks at Haggerty over the top of his glasses.

"Marcus Haggerty you are charged with a multitude of crimes including armed robbery, destroying government property, a prohibited weapons charge, and operating a space craft inside Earth's atmosphere without clearance."

"Since you were caught red handed by the Marines onboard the train, I can't imagine how you could even think of entering a not-guilty plea, but I am duty bound to ask. So, Mr. Haggerty, how do you plead?"

The prisoner does not respond at all, he says nothing, he doesn't move and even his facial expression doesn't change. He just stares at the judge with a cold, emotionless look on his face.

The judge asks again, "How do you plead, Mr. Haggerty?"

The lawyer looks at the prisoner then at the judge then back at the prisoner.

"You better say something."

The judge waits another minute and says, "Very well then. Your reluctance to respond to this court leaves me no choice. We will forego a trial of your peers and I will decide your fate myself. In light of all the evidences against you, I find you, Marcus Haggerty, guilty on all charges. I hereby sentence you to twenty years of hard labor on the penal asteroid P6421."

He bangs his gavel on the bench and says, "Bailiffs, take the prisoner away."

The bailiffs walk over to Haggerty, take him by the arms, stand him up, and lead him out the side door of the court room. They escort him back to the holding cell and sit him back down on the bench. They back out of the cell and activate the force field.

One bailiff pauses and says, "You just sit tight for about half an hour. We'll come get you when the transport to P6421 arrives."

Half an hour later the bailiff comes back with two armed guards and Carter Rayburn. The bailiff deactivates the cell's force field and steps out of the way. The two armed guards enter the cell and take the prisoner by the arms. They stand him up, walk him out of the cell and down the hall, followed closely by Carter. The four men walk down the long hallway and stop at the exterior security door. One guard swipes his security card, punches a code into the keypad, and leans down for a retinal scan. A buzzer sounds, the door unlocks, and slides open to the right, disappearing into the wall. The four men walk out onto the walkway that leads to the landing pad where the transport ship is waiting to take Haggerty to P6421.

The landing pad is in the center of a large secure compound, surrounded by a twenty-foot-high wall with guard towers at each of the four corners. Atop each guard tower there is a computer controlled quad barrel laser cannon turret. There are two armed guards in each of the towers and two more patrolling the walkway at the top of each wall.

A few seconds after the four men step out onto the walkway, they hear what sounds like a high-pitched screaming noise accompanied by a whoosh sound. A split second later the two closest guard towers explode, raining debris down into the compound. The four men crouch slightly and put their arms up above their heads to shield themselves from the falling debris.

A few seconds later, they hear the screaming noise and the whoosh sound again. The four men look up just in time to see two missiles scream in, seemingly from out of nowhere, and destroy the remaining two guard towers. Debris from the guard towers rains down into the compound.

Everyone in the compound and the guards on the walls are stunned and disoriented, their ears ringing from the noise from the explosions. It takes about twenty or thirty seconds for everyone to recover.

The guards grab Haggerty by the arms and to turn to go back into the courthouse when they hear the same noises again. They look up to see two more missiles scream in over the walls. The two missiles strike the rear of the transport ship and explode in two huge fireballs. Seconds later the entire ship explodes in a massive fireball. The concussion blows everyone off their feet and back several meters.

Carter, the two guards, and Haggerty are laying semi-conscious on the ground. They were far enough from the ship not to be killed by the explosion, but they are definitely injured from the concussion and from flying debris.

Carter slowly rolls over on his back and looks up to see a ship fly in over the wall and come to a stop about forty feet above him. A hatch opens on the bottom of the ship, two ropes drop out, and two men dressed in black assault fatigues repel down to the ground. The two men run over, grab the semi-conscious Haggerty, pick him up by the arms, and drag him over to the ropes. One man holds Haggerty up while the other puts a harness on him. They attach the ropes to their harnesses, then one of the men gives the ship the thumbs up signal. The ropes retract into the ship, pulling all three men up and inside. As soon as they are inside, the hatch closes, and the ship starts to move.

In his half-conscious state, Carter sees the door from the courthouse slide open and a guard runs out with a rocket launcher. The guard points the launcher at the ship and fires. The rocket streaks across the sky, but when it reaches the ship, there is no explosion.

Carter says to himself, "Must be a tracking device."

The ship accelerates, climbing rapidly, and is soon out of sight. As soon as the ship breaks orbit its FTL drive kicks in and the ship disappears in a bright blue flash of light.

Back at the courthouse, a force of medical and emergency personnel is arriving to help the wounded, put out fires, clean up the debris and to take care of those killed in the attack.

Carter loses consciousness just after he is picked up and placed on a medical gurney by two medics. They load him in an ambulance and take him to the hospital, luckily his injuries are not serious.

CHAPTER 8 - LET'S GO GET THEM

Back in Jasper, Nathan receives a call from the chief of police informing him of the attack on the courthouse. The chief orders Nathan and his crew to report to the Planetary Police headquarters in Seattle immediately. Nathan and his crew are in the hangar working on their ship when the call comes in.

"Okay everyone, listen up. There has been an attack on the courthouse in Seattle and we've been ordered to report to headquarters immediately. Go pack your things and report back here on the double. Wheels up in fifteen minutes."

Everyone rushes to their rooms to change into their duty uniforms and pack their belongings. Not even ten minutes later, Nathan and his crew have stowed their things in their cabins, they've secured the house and the hangar, and they are on the bridge getting the ship ready for takeoff.

"Ms. Arnoult, contact Jasper air traffic control and request clearance for a vertical takeoff."

"Aye sir."

A minute later Desiree says, "Sir, Jasper air traffic control has granted us clearance for a vertical takeoff, no traffic in the immediate area…. Captain."

This is the first time that any of the crew has called Nathan Captain and it caught him a little by surprise. He likes the sound of it, and he smiles just a little.

"Thank you, Ms. Arnoult."

"Mr. Bell, fire up the engines."

"Aye Captain."

The crew hears the jet engines spin up and start.

"Mr. Black, plot a course to Seattle."

"Aye Captain, course laid in."

"Take her up, Mr. Bell."

"Aye Captain."

Mr. Bell pushes the throttles halfway open and the ship rises. When the ship reaches two hundred feet, he adjusts the thrust vectoring, and the ship moves forward. Mr. Bell rams the throttles wide open after which the ship accelerates and climbs rapidly, pushing the crew back in their seats.

Nathan smiles knowing Mr. Bell loves to push the ship hard at takeoff both for fun and to toy with his crewmates.

After a couple of minutes Mr. Bell says, "Captain, we have reached an altitude of thirty thousand feet and we're cruising at six hundred and fifty knots. We should reach Seattle in about forty-five minutes."

"Thank you, Mr. Bell."

"Ms. Arnoult, please inform headquarters that we will arrive in about forty-five minutes."

"Aye Captain."

Nathan pushes a button on the command console on his chair. The front bridge window of the cruiser changes to view screen mode and plays the courthouse security footage from the time of the attack. The crew watches the whole thing from several camera angles. They see the missiles, the explosions, the deaths, the injuries, the ship and the escape. They also see the guard come out of the courthouse and fire the tracking device at the ship as it takes off across the sky. They continue to watch the video stream until medical and emergency personnel arrive and start helping the wounded.

Nathan spots a familiar face on the screen, so he freezes the image and zooms in. He was right, that was his best friend, Carter, on the screen being picked up and taken to an ambulance.

"Ms. Arnoult, please contact headquarters and find out which hospital Carter has been taken to for treatment and then contact the hospital to inquire about his condition."

"Aye Captain."

Nathan rewinds the security video and pauses it at a point where there is a clear view of the ship. He studies the ship and zooms in on several sections and markings. He also zooms in on the face of the prisoner that escaped and stares at the man's face for a minute.

Just then Desiree says, "Captain, Carter has been taken to the Northwest Hospital and Medical Center. He only suffered minor injuries and will be back on his feet in a week or so."

Relieved, Nathan says, "Thank you, Ms. Arnoult."

Forty-five minutes later, as their ship approaches Seattle, Nathan says, "Ms. Arnoult, contact Seattle air traffic control and request the approach vector and clearance for a vertical landing at the Planetary Police headquarters helipad."

"Aye Captain."

A minute later Ms. Arnoult says, "Captain, Seattle air traffic control has cleared us for a vertical landing at the Planetary Police headquarters helipad and has sent me the approach vector. I have sent the approach vector to Mr. Black's console."

"Thank you, Ms. Arnoult."

Mr. Black reviews the data and says, "Confirmed, approach vector laid in, Captain."

"Thank you, Mr. Black."

"Mr. Bell, take us down."

"Aye Captain."

Mr. Bell pulls back on the throttles, the ship descends, they break through the clouds and the vast city that is Seattle comes into view. As they approach Planetary Police headquarters, Mr. Bell slows the ship down and banks to port, turning around one hundred and eighty degrees. He slows the ship down to a crawl and lines it up with the helipad. Soon the ship is hovering at two hundred feet directly over the helipad. Mr. Bell pulls back on the throttles a little more and the ship descends slowly. When the ship reaches fifty feet, the landing gear comes down. Moments later the wheels touch the ground and Mr. Bell shuts the engines down.

Nathan stands up and says, "Nice smooth landing, Mr. Bell."

"Thank you, Captain."

The crew finishes powering down the ship and they make their way from the bridge down to the lower bay. Nathan opens the ramp, and the crew walks out onto the helipad.

The helipad ground crew are busy running around putting wheel chocks around the tires and checking out the new ship.

Nathan decides he doesn't want anyone poking around inside the ship, so he runs back up the ramp and grabs a small mobile computer from a storage locker and straps it on his wrist.

A voice comes from the computer and says, "Recognize, Captain Nathan Stone."

He runs back down the ramp, turns to face the ship and pushes a button on the computer. The ramp closes, and the crew hears a "chirp-chirp" sound and the landing lights flash.

Mr. Bell shakes his head, chuckles and says, "Seriously, you put a car alarm in the ship?"

Nathan smiles and says, "I did, but that's not all this little computer will do. This thing is a complete remote link to the ship with both touch and voice interface. We can do anything from here, even fire weapons. This system has many features including remote pickup. With just the push of one button, the ship will lift off, home in on this computer, and pick you up, as long as you're within a hundred miles of the ship."

The crew looks impressed by Nathan's tech toy, but they need to get into police headquarters for a briefing.

"Okay, let's get inside for our briefing with the chief."

They walk into the building and sign in with security via retinal scans. They follow Nathan into an elevator which takes them to the top floor of the building. As they exit the elevator, the chief's assistant greets them and guides them to a conference room. They all sit down around the conference room table and the chief's assistant brings in a large decanter full of coffee and a pitcher full of ice water. The crew helps themselves to the beverages and shortly thereafter the chief walks in to brief them.

"Good afternoon, everyone. Thank you for getting here so quickly. This attack caught us completely by surprise and we need all hands on deck for this one."

The chief sits down at the head of the conference room table and uses the touch panel interface in front of him to bring up Marcus Haggerty's record on the main view screen. They go through his record, which contains a long history of violent crime, starting when he was a teenager. Next the chief brings up the security footage from the attempted train robbery.

"Six or seven months ago, one of our listening posts on the edge of Earth's space intercepted a series of transmissions between Haggerty and an unknown party. The unknown party hired Haggerty and his team to steal a crate of rare ore from a military train transporting it from Seattle to Washington D.C. Working together with the EDF, we redirected the shipment of ore and set a trap Haggerty and his crew. We caught Haggerty, but his crew got away. Their ship achieved orbit and jumped into FTL before anyone could catch up to it to detain it."

Finally, the chief brings up the security footage from the attack on the courthouse. The chief pauses the video when the attacking ship flies into view.

"Anybody recognize that ship? It's the same ship from the attempted train robbery."

He continues to play the video through to the end where the guard come out of the courthouse with the rocket launcher and fires at the ship.

"As I'm sure you figured out, the guard did not fire a missile at the ship. He fired a tracking device that we affectionately refer to as a breadcrumb. It's a stealth device that attaches itself to the outside of a ship and it leaves a trail of radioactive micro transmitters that work quite simply like a trail of breadcrumbs."

Nathan asks the chief, "Do you think we could get half a dozen of these breadcrumbs for our new cruiser?"

The chief says, "Absolutely, Captain."

The chief nods to one of his aids, who walks over to the conference room door, pulls it open and waits.

Nathan says, "Ms. Norata, please go and oversee the transfer of six breadcrumbs to our ship."

"Aye Captain."

He then removes the small computer from his wrist and hands it to her.

"You'll need this to get into the ship."

Ms. Norata takes the small computer from Nathan and puts it on her wrist.

The computer says, "Recognize, Officer Aleena Norata.

Ms. Norata and the chief's aid walk out of the conference room and head down to the armory.

Nathan says, "The rest of you get back to the ship, fuel her up and make sure the food, water and weapons stores are full. I'm going to go visit Carter in the hospital to see if he can remember anything else that might be of use to us."

The rest of the crew stand and answer, "Aye Captain," in unison, then they leave the conference room.

Nathan and the chief stand and shake hands.

"Good luck, Captain Stone."

"Thank you, Chief."

Nathan leaves the conference room and takes an elevator down to the secure underground parking area where they keep the police cars. He approaches the first car in line and places his hand on the window of the driver's side door. Almost instantaneously a glowing green outline appears around his hand.

A voice comes from the front of the car and says, "Recognize, Captain Nathan Stone, access granted."

The door opens, pivoting up towards the front of the car.

Nathan jumps in the driver's seat and grabs the steering wheel, instantly all the cars systems come to life and the door closes.

The car's computerized voice says, "Hello, Captain Stone, what is your destination?"

"Northwest Hospital, Seattle."

"Destination found and route laid in. Would you like me to drive?"

"No, I'd like to drive."

"Very well."

Nathan steps on the accelerator pedal, maybe a little too much, as the car's back tires spin, screech and smoke. Being an old school, classic muscle car enthusiast, who owns several cars with over five hundred horsepower, Nathan is surprised and impressed with the power that this electric police car has. He quickly exits the underground parking area and turns right on the street in front of the police headquarters. He touches a button on the touch panel in the dash to turn on the siren and the red and blue flashing lights. He changes to the left lane, steps on the accelerator and flies past all the cars that have pulled over to the right-hand lane to let him pass. In no time at all he is pulling into the hospital parking lot. He parks the car close to the front doors in a spot designated for police cars, gets out, and makes his way into the hospital.

Upon entering the hospital, he stops at a wall panel computer and asks it for Carter's room number. The computer tells him the number and displays a map that shows the most direct route to that room. Nathan quickly makes his way to Carter's room and peeks in the window before entering. He sees Carter lying on the bed asleep looking kind of beat up, battered, bruised and bandaged. He opens the door, walks in, quietly pulls a chair up to the right side of the bed and sits down.

Carter must have sensed his presence because within a minute he wakes, opens his eyes and turns his head to see his best friend sitting there.

Nathan smiles, "Hey buddy, you must be slipping in your old age, you got your ass kicked and you let the bad guy get away."

Carter chuckles and shakes his head, "Oh, it's like that is it"?

Nathan smiles and says, "So tell me all about this case."

"Not much to tell really, we intercepted some radio transmissions that told us all we needed to know. The who, what, where, why, when, and how of a robbery in the making."

"Your old buddy Captain Creeksto hired this group of cold, ruthless criminals, led by Marcus Haggerty, to steal a box of ore that was mined on a small planet called Trynx 3 from a military train. We setup a sting and captured Haggerty, but his ship and crew got away. Obviously, they wanted him back."

Nathan says, "Captain Creeksto and Trynx 3 again, huh?"

Carter asks, "What's so special about this ore from Trynx 3 and why does Creeksto want it so badly?"

"I'm not sure, but I'm going to find out. You stay here, heal up and flirt with the nurses. See you soon."

Nathan gets up and turns to go out the door.

Carter says, "Nathan, be careful. These are some really bad men and the Sulari are known for being ruthless scum bags."

Nathan smiles at Carter, nods, and exits the room. He heads back to his police car and drives back to police headquarters. He parks the police car back in the secure underground parking area and heads back upstairs to see the chief before going after the criminals. Nathan knocks on the chief's open door as he walks in.

"Hey Chief, Carter just filled me in on this case. Your unknown party is Captain Creeksto of the Sulari. This is the second time Creeksto has tried to get his hands on this ore from Trynx 3."

"How do you know this, Captain Stone?"

"I had a run in with Creeksto on my last mission aboard the Invincible."

"The EDF failed to share that tidbit of information with us."

"Sir, if Creeksto wants this ore so badly, might I suggest contacting the EDF to send the Invincible to guard Trynx 3? I wouldn't put it past Creeksto, at this point, to sneak through Earth's space to try to steal some of that ore."

"Good thinking, Captain. I'll call Admiral Hollister to see if he'll dispatch the Invincible."

"Might I also suggest we find out what is so special about this ore?"

"I'll see what I can find out about this ore. What's so special about it and why Creeksto wants it so badly."

"Thank you, sir. I'll keep you updated on our progress."

"Good hunting, Captain Stone."

Nathan leaves the chief's office, makes his way out of the building, and back to the helipad. When he gets there, he finds his crew hard at work loading up the ship with everything they need including food, water, diesel fuel for the ATV, and aviation fuel for the fighter and shuttle. They are also topping up the ammunition and missile stores just in case this is a prolonged mission. The ground crew is refueling the ship itself and performing a pre-launch inspection.

Nathan walks up to Mr. Black who is overseeing the resupply and asks, "How long until we can take off, Mr. Black?"

"Five minutes, Captain. We're just about done."

"Excellent, we'll leave in ten minutes. I'll be on the bridge."

"Aye Captain."

Nathan walks up the ramp into the lower bay of the ship and makes his way up to the bridge. When he enters the bridge, he finds Ms. Norata at the tactical station entering the security codes to the bread crumb into her console so they can track Haggerty's ship. As soon as she's done, a hologram appears over her station showing Earth and the surrounding quadrants of space. A few seconds later, the trail of breadcrumbs appears as small, bright, orange dots.

Ms. Norata says, "Captain, we're receiving the breadcrumb's transmissions and tracking their ship. They have a bit of a head start on us, but we'll find them."

"Great work, Ms. Norata. These breadcrumbs are amazing pieces of technology."

"They sure are, Captain."

Nathan takes a seat in his chair and then asks Ms. Norata, "Can you transfer the tracking hologram to my position?"

"Aye Captain."

She presses two buttons on her console and then the hologram appears in front of Nathan. Nathan sits there studying it for a minute and then reaches his hands into the hologram. Then by moving his hands farther apart, he makes the hologram zoom in. Now he can see the last three breadcrumbs in the trail up close. Soon a fourth bread crumb appears.

Nathan says, "There you are, you son of a bitch, I've got you now."

The rest of the crew files in and takes their positions.

Mr. Black is the last one in and he says, "We are all loaded up and the ramp is secured, Captain."

"Excellent, thank you, Mr. Black."

"Ms. Arnoult, contact Seattle air traffic control and request clearance for a vertical takeoff, then contact Earth space flight control and request clearance for space flight."

"Aye Captain."

A few minutes later she says, "Captain, Seattle air traffic control has granted us clearance for a vertical takeoff. No traffic in the immediate area. Earth space flight control has also given us clearance for space flight."

"Thank you, Ms. Arnoult."

"Mr. Bell, fire up the engines."

"Aye Captain."

The crew hears the jet engines spin up and start.

"Mr. Black, plot a course heading two seven zero degrees, due west out over the Pacific."

"Aye Captain, course laid in."

"Take her up, Mr. Bell."

"Aye Captain."

Mr. Bell pushes the throttles halfway open and the ship rises. When the ship reaches two hundred feet, he spins the ship one hundred and eighty degrees and adjusts the thrust vectoring, so the ship moves forward. As soon as they have cleared the city, Mr. Bell rams the throttles wide open, after which the ship accelerates and climbs rapidly. In just a few minutes, the sky turns black around them and the stars appear as they approach the edge of the atmosphere. At this point Mr. Bell disengages the jet engines and closes the air intakes. He then engages the sub-light engines and rams the throttles wide open. The ship accelerates, almost violently, to achieve escape velocity.

The ship's computer announces in its female voice, "Now leaving Earth's gravity. Artificial gravity plating is coming online."

As soon as they break orbit Nathan says, "Mr. Black, plot a course following the trail of breadcrumbs."

"Aye Captain, course laid in."

"Mr. Bell, engage the FTL drive. Speed 14 TSL."

"Aye Captain."

The ship accelerates rapidly away from earth and soon the crew sees the bright blue flash of light through the bridge windows as the ship enters FTL.

A few minutes later Mr. Bell says, "Captain, we have reached 14 TSL."

"Thank you, Mr. Bell."

Nathan reaches his hands into the outside edges of the tracking hologram in front of him, and then brings his hands together, causing the hologram to zoom out so Nathan can see the entire trail of breadcrumbs. At the beginning of the trail, there is now a red dot showing the position of their police cruiser.

Nathan thinks to himself, "They've got a good head start on us. It'll take a couple of days to catch up to them, but we will."

Nathan says, "Well, there is no point in sitting here watching these dots. It will take us a few days to catch up to them so let's use this time productively. Let's go and get settled into our quarters and then we'll prep the shuttle, the fighter and the ATV so they are ready should we need them."

The crew answer in unison, "Aye Captain."

One by one they leave the bridge to go to their quarters.

They all spend the next six hours settling into their quarters, prepping the shuttle, the fighter and the ATV for action. When finished they all meet in the galley for dinner. The mood on the ship is one of excitement, as this is their first real mission as a team. They're all laughing and having a good time during dinner. Once dinner is done, they head back up to the bridge to check the systems before heading off to bed.

Nathan and Desiree are the first ones to say goodnight and head to their quarters. Since they are officially a couple now, they are sharing the largest cabin on the ship. The rest of the crew remains on the bridge to sit and talk for a while before heading to bed. About ten minutes after Nathan and Desiree leave, a red light flashes, and an alarm buzzes on Mr. Nagata's engineering console.

Mr. Nagata says, "That's funny, the gravity plating in the captain's cabin has failed. I better get down there and check it out."

Ms. Norata giggles and says, "Oh believe me Chief, you don't want to go down there."

Mr. Nagata looks at her and says, "What do you mean? The captain and Desiree could be in trouble."

Ms. Norata says, "Oh, they're not in trouble. Well maybe Desiree is."

The others chuckle just a little.

Mr. Nagata looks at her, still puzzled.

Ms. Norata tilts her head a little, smiles and says, "They're having zero gravity sex."

Mr. Nagata smiles and says, "Oooooooooooh," and then turns back to his console and silences the alarm.

The four of them have a good laugh and then one by one head off to bed leaving the ship's automated systems in charge for the night.

CHAPTER 9 - A LITTLE BACKWATER PLANET

The next morning the crew is awake early, and one by one they wander into the galley for breakfast. The last to arrive are Nathan and Desiree who are met with knowing smiles and giggles from the other crew members. Desiree grabs a few things for breakfast and sits down at the table. She looks across the table to see Aleena siting there, elbows on the table, arms crossed, with a big smile on her face. Desiree's eyes shift between her food and Aleena several times.

Aleena leans forward and silently mouths the word, "Well?"

Desiree's face flushes slightly with embarrassment, but then she smiles and mouths the word, "Amazing," back to Aleena.

Just then Nathan joins them, sitting down beside Desiree with his breakfast and coffee. He looks at both women and sees the big smiles on their faces. Not wanting to make Nathan suspicious, they both stop smiling, Aleena leans back in her chair and tries to act nonchalant.

Nathan realizes he interrupted something. He feels a little uncomfortable, so he quickly finishes his breakfast, grabs his coffee and gets up to go to the bridge. Just before exiting the galley he looks back to see Aleena smiling knowingly at him. He just smiles, shakes his head and walks out.

When Nathan gets to the bridge, he sits down and brings up the tracking hologram. The first thing he notices is the display has changed slightly. He expected to see a bunch of breadcrumbs, but instead there are only a few crumbs leading to a flashing orange dot.

Nathan says to himself, "They must have landed somewhere," so he puts his hands into the center of the hologram and then swipes out towards the edges, making the image zoom in.

He zooms in several times until he can see a solar system that has twelve planets, on the edge of a brightly colored nebula. The flashing orange dot is on the northern hemisphere of the sixth planet. Nathan touches the sixth planet with his finger making the hologram zoom right in it. It also displays the name of the planet, Cyrus 6, displays the coordinates of the breadcrumb on the surface, and shows him a summary of the planet.

The summary says, "Cyrus 6 is a backwater planet on the edge of Earth's sector of space. The planet has one settlement with approximately two thousand inhabitants who consist mostly of farmers and their families. The planet's spaceport is a haven for criminals, smugglers, and other seedy types because it's so far out on the edge. Neither the EDF nor the Planetary Police have a presence there."

A few minutes later, the rest of the crew join him on the bridge.

Before they can all sit down Nathan says, "They've landed on a planet."

The crew gathers around Nathan's chair to read the summary for Cyrus 6.

After everyone has read the summary Nathan says, "Okay, here's what we're going to do. We'll cloak the ship on approach to the planet, just in case somebody is watching. We'll set the ship down outside the settlement and then drive into town in the ATV. Nine times out of ten there is a seedy bar not far from the spaceport on these little back water planets, so we'll start our search there. Mr. Black, Ms. Norata, go prep the ATV for action."

Mr. Black and Ms. Norata both say, "Aye Captain," and then head down to the lower bay where the ATV is stored.

"Ms. Arnoult, update the police chief on our progress. Let him know that we've tracked them to Cyrus 6."

"Aye Captain."

"Let's just hope they're not switching ships on us."

Nathan thinks for a minute then pushes a button on his command console to activate the internal comm system.

"Ms. Norata, throw two breadcrumbs in the ATV just in case they switch ships on us."

Down in the lower bay, Ms. Norata walks over to the comm panel on the wall, pushes a button and says, "Will do, Captain."

She walks over to the armory door, keys in the code to unlock it, goes in and grabs two breadcrumb launchers. She puts the breadcrumbs in the back of the ATV along with the small arms, explosives, food, water, two med kits, and two cans of extra fuel that she and Mr. Black had already loaded. When they are all done loading up the ATV, they head back up to the bridge.

Upon entering the bridge Ms. Norata says, "Captain, the ATV is loaded and ready for action."

"Thank you, Ms. Norata, Mr. Black."

"Now all we can do is wait. We'll arrive in just a little over nine hours."

The next eight hours pass very slowly. Even though they are traveling at speeds that most people cannot even begin to comprehend, our little section of the galaxy is so vast that it can still take a long time to get to where you need to go. The crew spends the time checking the ships systems, monitoring the sensors, talking and laughing, they even watch another old science fiction movie on the main view screen while they eat lunch.

After eight long hours, Nathan finally says, "Okay everyone, suit up. We land in one hour."

The crew answers in unison, "Aye Captain," and then they head to their quarters to change.

They change into their black assault fatigues and tactical vests, grab their side arms, taser gloves, tactical night vision glasses, collapsible batons, and a few personal, close quarter weapons. When they are dressed and ready, they head back up to the bridge and take their stations.

Mr. Bell says, "Captain, we will arrive at Cyrus 6 in fifteen minutes."

"Thank you, Mr. Bell."

Fifteen minutes later Nathan says, "Mr. Bell, drop us out of FTL."

"Aye Captain."

The crew sees a bright blue flash of light through the bridge windows as the ship drops out of FTL.

Cyrus 6 and the nebula instantly appear in the bridge windows.

"Ms. Norata, engage the cloaking device."

"Aye Captain, engaging the cloaking device now."

"Mr. Bell, take us down and land north of the settlement behind the cover of the hills."

"Aye Captain."

The ship's nose drops and soon they are entering the atmosphere of the planet. Mr. Bell brings her in for a vertical landing just where Nathan requested, to the north of the settlement behind some hills. After they have landed, the crew takes a few minutes to shut down the ship's systems.

When they are finished, Nathan stands up and says, "Okay, everyone, let's go."

One by one they exit the bridge, head to the lower bay, and jump into the ATV.

Nathan is the last to get in the ATV as he stopped to put on one of the small mobile wrist computers. Nathan presses a button on his wrist computer and the ramp opens. Mr. Bell drives the ATV out of the ship and then Nathan presses the button again to close the ramp. They have left the cloaking device on to hide the ship as they don't want to risk alerting anyone to their presence.

It's about a fifteen minute drive to the spaceport. It's dark out, so as they approach, they turn off the headlights on the ATV, approaching slowly and with stealth. It doesn't take them long to spot Haggerty's ship sitting on one of the pads. The ship looks to be powered down and the rear entry ramp has been left open.

"Stop here, Mr. Bell. Let's sit and surveil the ship for a while to see if anyone comes back."

Mr. Bell says, "Aye Captain," and shuts the engine off.

Before too long, they see a man approach the ship and walk up the open ramp. The man is inside for just a few minutes before he emerges and exits the spaceport, walking east. The team gives him a bit of a head start before they follow him. They want to make sure he doesn't spot them and run. The man walks a few blocks and enters a rather seedy looking bar.

Nathan says, "Hey look at that, a bad guy going into a seedy looking bar just outside a spaceport on a little backwater planet. Was I right or was I right? Mr. Bell, let's back into the alley there across from the bar."

Mr. Bell says, "Aye Captain," and then parks the ATV in the alley.

The team exits the ATV and gathers on the passenger side for direction.

"Okay, Mr. Nagata, I want you to launch four surveillance drones to watch all sides of the bar. The rest of you come with me."

Mr. Nagata says, "Aye Captain," then opens the back of the ATV, and grabs the case with the drones in it.

He takes the drones and the control tablet out, programs in where he wants them to go, and sends them on their way. The drones' night vision camera feeds show up on the control tablet with incredible clarity, impressing Mr. Nagata. He climbs into the driver's seat of the ATV to wait and monitor.

The rest of the team walks across the street and enters the bar. They stop just inside the entrance to scan the room for Haggerty. There are several steps down into the bar, so the team is above everyone making it easier to look around. There is all manner of unsavory looking people in the bar. There is music playing, and everyone is speaking loudly to be heard, so the noise level is quite high. The team looks around to see if they can spot the man they followed in, but they don't see him.

Next, they use the facial recognition feature on their tactical glasses to find Haggerty in the bar full of people, but they do not find him. The next step is to canvas the bar with his picture to see if something shakes loose. Some patrons notice that there are five Planetary Police officers standing in the bar's entrance. Soon most of the bar has turned to look at them. Then someone shuts the music off. You could now hear a pin drop in the bar. The team feels a little unnerved.

Nathan steps forward and says, "Good evening folks. Sorry to interrupt your fun. We are looking for a man named Marcus Haggerty. My officers are going to walk around and show you an image of him and we would appreciate your cooperation in helping us locate him."

The team walks down the steps into the bar, splits up and begins showing the patrons an image of Haggerty using small, handheld, holographic projectors. Nathan stays at the entrance and observes the patrons for any suspicious or potentially dangerous behavior.

Desiree approaches a table with three men sitting at it and asks, "Have any of you seen this man, Marcus Haggerty?"

Two of them, rather large men, stand up on either side of Desiree.

The third man stays seated and says, "You and the other officers should leave now if you know what's good for you. We don't like cops around here."

This catches Nathan's attention, so he puts his hand on his holstered blaster and steps down one step into the bar.

Desiree looks at the seated man and says, "We'll leave when we find Haggerty, not before."

The seated man says, "Okay, I gave you a chance," and then snaps his fingers.

The two large men take a step towards Desiree, but to Nathan's surprise she doesn't look scared. Not even a little bit. She has a smile on her face. An evil smile.

With lightning speed, Desiree jumps up, spins and strikes the man closest to her in the jaw with a hook kick. The man is out cold before he hits the ground. It's more than likely that when he wakes up, he will find he is missing a few teeth. The instant Desiree lands from her kick, she drops, spins, and sweeps the other man's feet out from under him with a dragon's tail sweep. The man's feet fly up, he falls back, and smacks his head on the table behind him. He too is unconscious before he hits the ground. When he wakes up, he's going to have one hell of a headache.

Desiree turns and says to the seated man, "Is that the best you've got?"

Nathan's eyes and mouth are wide open in disbelief, he's in shock. He can't believe that his little Desiree effortlessly took out those two large men.

He looks across the bar at Mr. Black and they both shrug their shoulders and exchange looks as if to say, "Did you know she could do that?"

Nathan and the other team members converge on Desiree's position. The man seated at the table stands up, smiles, and snaps his fingers again. Obviously, this guy is the boss man. Fifteen men stand up and look menacingly at the five police officers.

The team forms a circle with their backs facing inwards. All but Nathan draw their collapsible batons and snap them open. Nathan reaches back and pulls a two-foot-long silver pipe out of the back of his tactical vest. He pushes a button in the middle of the pipe which makes the ends extend into a six-foot-long bow staff. He spins the bow a few times and then draws it close to his side.

Ten of the fifteen men are approaching the team, the other five are hanging back. Nathan has three men that have set their sights on him.

Nathan can feel his heart rate rising and the adrenaline coursing through his body. He uses a deep breathing technique that was taught to him by one of his martial arts instructors to calm himself and focus.

Nathan's team is well trained to handle situations exactly like this, but the threat they are under still causes adrenaline to flood their systems.

Nathan locks eyes with the biggest, meanest looking one and says, "Trust me, you don't want to do this."

The man says, "Yes, we do, cop."

Nathan doesn't wait after hearing that. He jumps up, spins and hits the big man square in the solar plexus with a back kick.

This knocks the man flying back about ten feet, destroying a table and a chair when he lands. The man does not get up. A split second later Nathan hits the second man in the face with a front kick, knocking him flying. Then Nathan pivots slightly and throws a side kick at the third man, catching him square in the jaw. Nathan's kick takes him right off his feet and knocks him unconscious.

At this point the bar fight is in full swing, but Nathan's team handles the untrained thugs with ease. Mr. Black, Mr. Bell and Ms. Norata take out several men with their batons.

Desiree takes out another man by first striking him square in the chest with a back kick. Then she jumps into the air, catches his head between her thighs and uses her body weight to throw him as she twists and falls to the floor. After that she renders him unconscious with her taser gloves. When Desiree stands up another man grabs her by the arm, spins her around to face him, and raises his fist to strike her.

Nathan sees this, and with lightning speed, draws his blaster and stuns the man. The stun blast causes the man to fly back and crash through a window, landing outside on the sidewalk.

Just like that, the first ten men are all lying on the ground unconscious, and the five police officers didn't get a scratch on them.

The other five men that were hanging back put their hands up at shoulder height and back away as if to say, "We want no part of this anymore."

The team puts their weapons away and surrounds the boss man. Nathan pulls out his small handheld holographic projector and again shows the man an image of Haggerty.

"I'm going to ask you one more time. Have you seen Marcus Haggerty?"

The boss man says, "Okay, I sold Haggerty and his crew a new ship. They're prepping it to leave right now."

Just then, the man the team followed into the bar walks in from an adjoining room in the back of the building. He sees the five police officers, panics and runs out the back door.

Nathan pushes a button on his radio and says, "Mr. Nagata, there is a man running out the back door, tail him with a drone."

"Aye Captain, I've got him."

Nathan and the team head to the front door, but just before exiting the bar, Nathan turns around and says to everyone, "Sorry for interrupting your fun and for making a mess of your bar. Enjoy the rest of your evening, folks."

The team heads back to the ATV, they jump in and head for the spaceport.

Mr. Nagata is busy watching the man that ran from the bar on the drone control tablet. He watches the man run through a hangar to a ship sitting outside on a pad. There are five other men working around the ship who appear to be prepping it for take-off. When the man runs up, the other five men converge on him. He is most likely telling them about the police he saw in the bar. The men then fan out around the ship, and it appears that they have gone back to prepping the ship for take-off, but with greater urgency.

Mr. Nagata presses the button to activate the facial recognition program. The drone's camera zooms in on each of the men's faces and takes a picture. It runs the pictures through the database, and a few seconds later shows a positive match for Marcus Haggerty.

"Captain, the drone has identified Haggerty. He's prepping his new ship on pad twenty-one alpha."

"Excellent, let's go get him."

The team jumps out of the ATV and gathers at the rear doors. Nathan hands each one of them a pulse rifle and directs them where to go. Ms. Norata grabs a bread crumb from the back of the ATV and slings it over her back.

She looks at Nathan and says, "Just in case they get off the ground."

"Good thinking."

The team makes their way into the spaceport and approach Haggerty's ship from behind with stealth. They fan out in a one-hundred-and-eighty-degree pattern and take up positions behind the various crates and small vehicles sitting along the edge of the pad. The team takes a few minutes to observe the six men that are hurrying to get the ship ready to take-off, to make sure there won't be any surprises. Nathan signals his team to check readiness. They all signal back that they are ready.

Nathan yells, "MARCUS HAGGERTY, THIS IS THE PLANETARY POLICE! THROW DOWN YOUR WEAPONS AND LAY DOWN ON THE GROUND!"

Haggerty yells back, "I DON'T THINK SO!"

He then pulls his blaster from its holster and starts shooting in Nathan's direction. Haggerty's five men pull their blasters and start shooting as well. At this point laser blasts are flying and there are small explosions everywhere around Nathan.

Haggerty yells, "INTO THE SHIP! LET'S GET OUT OF HERE!"

Nathan yells, "OPEN FIRE! DON'T LET THEM GET IN THE SHIP!"

The team opens fire on Haggerty's men with their pulse rifles, which have a significantly higher rate of fire than the average blaster pistol. The barrage sends Haggerty's men diving for cover behind anything close to them. Nathan's team has them pinned down. Laser blasts are hitting the ship, crates, barrels, the tug vehicle, and the forklift that Haggerty's men have taken cover behind. Small explosions rain sparks and debris down on them with each laser blast. Haggerty's men are only getting off the occasional shot at Nathan's team. Haggerty realizes they can't do this all night. They have to move.

He yells, "GET TO THE SHIP!"

His men jump to their feet and run for the ramp at the rear of the ship, shooting at Nathan's team wildly as they run.

Nathan's team concentrates their fire on the ramp, but the first two men make it up the ramp and into the ship. The third man was not so lucky. He catches a laser blast in the thigh and falls on the ramp. The fourth and fifth man run up the ramp, grab the injured man, and start dragging him up the ramp into the ship. The fifth man catches a laser blast in the mid-section and is blown right off the ramp onto the ground. The fourth man drags the injured man up the ramp to safety inside the ship.

Now the only one left outside is Haggerty, so he jumps up and starts running for the ramp. He is really fast. The team tries their best to shoot him, but amazingly, Haggerty traverses the intense laser blast barrage and makes it up the ramp, closing it behind him.

Nathan yells, "TAKE OUT THE ENGINES! DON'T LET THAT SHIP TAKE OFF!"

The team blasts the ship's jet engines as they start up, but the armor is too strong for their pulse rifles to cut through. The jet engines go to full power, the VTOL diverters drop, directing the thrust down at the ground, and the ship lifts off the pad.

Nathan sees Ms. Norata throw her pulse rifle on the ground and unsling the breadcrumb launcher from her back. She pulls the launch tube to extend it and flips the end covers open. She drops to one knee, aims and fires the missile.

The missile chases the ship across the sky and makes contact just as the ship pulls up dramatically and climbs for the heavens. As soon as the ship breaks orbit, they engage their FTL drive and are gone.

Ms. Norata looks at the screen on the launcher's control box. It shows the breadcrumb is attached and operating normally.

She yells, "GOT THEM! THE TRACKER IS ACTIVE!"

Nathan yells, "EXCELLENT! EVERYONE BACK TO THE ATV!"

Nathan pushes the pickup button on his small, remote, wrist computer.

Miles away the computer on board the police cruiser receives the pickup request and begins its automated launch procedures. The jet engines fire up, the cloak disengages, the red and blue police lights begin flashing, and the landing lights come on. When the engines have finished spooling up to full power, the VTOL diverters drop, and the ship lifts off. It ascends to two hundred feet, the landing gear retracts, the ship changes from vertical mode to flight mode and takes off towards the spaceport.

Nathan and the team get back to the ATV and store their weapons in the back. Mr. Nagata recalls the four drones, puts them back in the case, and throws them in the back of the ATV. They jump into the ATV and drive to a clear area just outside of the settlement to wait for the ship to arrive.

In just a few short minutes, they see the flashing red and blue lights and the landing lights coming towards them at high speed. The ship slows as it gets closer to them, the landing gear comes down, and the ship switches from flight mode to vertical mode. The ship touches down gently about twenty yards from the ATV. Nathan pushes a button on his small, remote wrist computer to open the entry ramp to the lower bay. They drive the ATV into the bay, shut it down, secure it for flight, and then close the entry ramp. The crew rushes up to the bridge and quickly takes their positions.

"Okay, Mr. Bell, let's go get them."

"Aye Captain."

Mr. Bell pushes the throttles halfway open and the ship rises. When the ship reaches two hundred feet, he adjusts the thrust vectoring, so the ship moves forward. A few seconds later, Mr. Bell rams the throttles wide open and pulls the nose up. The ship blasts away from the surface, climbing rapidly towards the heavens.

Inside the cruiser, the crew is experiencing high g-forces from their extreme take-off. They are pinned back into their seats and can hardly lift their arms. In just a few minutes, the sky turns black around them and the stars appear as they approach the edge of the atmosphere. At this point Mr. Bell disengages the jet engines and closes the air intakes. He then engages the sub-light engines and rams the throttles wide open. The ship accelerates, almost violently, to achieve escape velocity.

The ship's computer announces in its female voice, "Now leaving Cyrus 6's gravity. Artificial gravity plating is coming online."

As soon as they break orbit Nathan says, "Mr. Black, plot a course following the trail of breadcrumbs."

"Aye Captain, course laid in."

"Mr. Bell, engage the FTL drive, speed 14 TSL."

"Aye Captain."

The ship accelerates rapidly and soon the crew sees a bright blue flash of light through the bridge windows as the ship enters FTL.

A few minutes later Mr. Bell announces, "Captain, we have reached 14 TSL and we're following the breadcrumbs."

"Thank you, Mr. Bell."

CHAPTER 10 - THE NEPTUNE ONE

Haggerty only has a slight lead on Nathan and his team, but that's about to change.

About an hour into the pursuit Desiree suddenly sits upright and says, "Captain, we're receiving a distress call."

"On speakers."

"Aye Captain."

"This is the Earth freighter Neptune One. We are under attack by an unknown vessel. Our shields are down, we have a hull breach, and our weapons and engines have been disabled. I think they mean to board us. We are broadcasting our coordinates. Any vessels in the area, we need help."

"Mr. Black, do you have the coordinates?"

"I have them, Captain, laying in a course."

"Mr. Bell, change course to intercept."

"Aye Captain."

"Mr. Black, time to intercept?"

"Eight minutes, Captain."

"Ms. Arnoult, open a channel."

"Channel open, Captain."

"Neptune One, this is Earth Planetary Police Zero One Niner, Captain Nathan Stone speaking. We are en route to your position, ETA eight minutes."

"Thank you, Captain Stone. Please hurry, they're going to board us."

"Acknowledged, Captain, we'll be there ASAP."

"Ms. Arnoult, continue to monitor transmissions."

"Aye Captain."

"Ms. Norata, shields up in inductive mode, and bring the weapons systems online."

"Aye Captain, shields up in inductive mode, and the weapons are online."

Just then Desiree interrupts, "Captain, I think they've been boarded. I can hear people yelling on the freighter and I can hear laser blasts. I just heard a loud scream, a small explosion and then the channel went dead."

"Thank you, Ms. Arnoult."

The crew can see that Nathan is eager to get there to help the people on the freighter. He's sitting on the edge of his seat and he's fidgeting a lot.

"Mr. Black, time to intercept?"

"Six minutes, Captain."

"Mr. Bell, I want you to drop us out of FTL right on top of them, so whoever it is doesn't have time to raise their shields."

"Aye Captain."

"Ms. Norata, as soon as we drop out of FTL, I want you to lock a full spread of missiles on the attacking ship's engines and fire."

"Aye Captain."

A few minutes later Mr. Bell says, "Approaching the freighters coordinates. Dropping out of FTL in three... two... one..."

There is a bright blue flash of light through the bridge windows and then the freighter and a large, dark, ominous looking ship appear directly in front of them, about two hundred and fifty yards away. Mr. Bell dropped them out of light speed exactly where they needed to be.

Nathan says, "That's a Sulari ship."

Ms. Norata says, "Target locked, firing."

Four missiles fire from the wings of the police cruiser and streak towards the engines of the Sulari ship. Nathan pushes a button on the command console on his chair, after which the main front window of the cruiser changes to view screen mode and displays the freighter, the Sulari ship and the missiles.

"Mr. Bell, put some distance between us and the Sulari ship."

"Aye Captain."

Mr. Bell pulls the nose of the police cruiser up and banks away from the Sulari ship to get clear. As their ship turns away the main view screen automatically displays the side and then aft view. The crew sees all four missiles impact on the engines of the Sulari ship followed by large explosions that cause massive amounts of damage.

The force of the missiles impacting, and subsequent explosions, exerts enough force to break the docking seal and separate the two ships. The crew sees several Sulari get sucked out into the vacuum of space from both ships before the computers can close the airlocks. The Sulari ship is now drifting out of control.

"Mr. Bell, bring us around for another pass."

"Aye Captain."

He turns the ship around one hundred and eighty degrees to start his run when suddenly the Sulari ship opens fire with its main laser cannons.

"Mr. Bell, evasive maneuvers."

"Aye Captain."

He rolls the ship to port and drops it under the laser blasts. Mr. Bell is an incredible pilot and maneuvers the police cruiser to dodge most of the laser blasts. The shields absorb the rest.

"Ms. Norata, arm the Gatling lasers and take out those laser cannon turrets."

"Aye Captain, targets acquired, firing."

The Gatling lasers in the wings of the police cruiser light up throwing sixty bursts per second. They cut two of the four main laser cannon turrets to pieces.

As the police cruiser passes underneath the Sulari ship Nathan says, "Ms. Norata, lock missiles on the two remaining laser cannon turrets and fire."

"Aye Captain, missiles locked, firing."

Four more missiles streak away from the wings of the police cruiser, heading straight out in front of them. The missiles then pull up sharply turning around one hundred and eighty degrees, streaking back past the police cruiser towards the Sulari ship. The main view screen is again displaying the aft view, so the crew sees four large explosions as the missiles impact, destroying the other two laser cannon turrets.

"Ms. Arnoult, signal the Sulari vessel and ask for their surrender."

"Aye Captain."

Desiree activates ship to ship communications and says, "Sulari vessel, this is Earth Planetary Police Zero One Niner. We have disabled your engines and destroyed your main weapons. You are ordered to surrender your vessel."

Moments later Desiree says, "Captain, I received a one-word response from the Sulari. They simply said, 'Never', sir."

"Thank you, Ms. Arnoult."

Just then a multitude of smaller laser turrets on the Sulari ship fire at the police cruiser, but these are easily handled by the shields. It's clear the Sulari will have to be dealt with, as Nathan and his crew can't begin rescue operations until the threat has been removed.

"Mr. Bell, bring us about one hundred and eighty degrees and then come to a full stop."

"Aye Captain."

He turns the police cruiser until the Sulari ship is in front of them once again and then comes to a full stop.

"Captain, the helm is showing all stop, two kilometers to target."

"Thank you, Mr. Bell."

"Ms. Norata, scan for their main reactor and lock onto it with the particle beam weapons."

"Aye Captain, target locked."

"Fire."

"Aye Captain, firing particle beams now."

Two red sparkling beams erupt from the tips of the wings, slicing right through the Sulari ship like a hot knife through butter. When the beams reach the reactor core, it explodes in a massive fireball which vaporizes the ship.

"Ms. Norata, scan for other ships in the area and for ships approaching in FTL."

"Aye Captain, scanning now."

After a minute she says, "Captain, no other ships in the area and nothing approaching in FTL."

"Thank you, Ms. Norata."

"Mr. Bell, go prep the shuttle for launch."

Mr. Bell says, "Aye Captain," then he quickly exits the bridge, heading for the rear bay.

Nathan says, "Mr. Black, come with me."

"Aye Captain."

As Nathan and Mr. Black exit the bridge, Nathan says, "Ms. Norata, you have the con."

Ms. Norata says, "Aye Captain," then she walks over and sits down at Mr. Bell's station.

Nathan and Mr. Black head down to the armory in the lower bay. Nathan enters the code to unlock the armory, they walk in and stand in front of the two Gen 4 armored exo-suits.

Nathan looks at Mr. Black and says, "Time to take these things for a test drive."

Mr. Black smiles and says, "Oh yes sir, Captain."

It takes them about fifteen minutes to get into the suits and power them up. When they are ready, they head towards the rear bay of the police cruiser where Mr. Bell is getting the shuttle ready for launch. In the rear bay, Mr. Bell can hear their footsteps as they approach. The suits are rather heavy, so with each step there is a loud metallic thud that reverberates through the ship. Nathan and Mr. Black walk into the bay and head for the shuttle. Mr. Bell guides them through the side door of the shuttle. The suits are bulky, so they barely fit through the door.

Once Nathan and Mr. Black are in, Mr. Bell jumps in the pilot's seat and closes the side door. He opens the shuttle bay doors and pushes the throttles up a little. The shuttle lifts off the deck, Mr. Bell nudges it forward, and a few seconds later the shuttle passes through the atmospheric force field and out into space. Immediately after exiting the bay, Mr. Bell turns and heads for the freighter. When they get close to the freighter, he slows the shuttle down to a crawl. He then rotates the shuttle one hundred and eighty degrees to align the docking port, which is in the rear of the shuttle, with the docking port on the side of the freighter. Then Mr. Bell engages the laser guided auto-dock system. The shuttle's computer takes over and aligns itself with the freighter's docking port using the maneuvering thrusters. A minute later, the shuttle makes contact with the freighter. The three men hear a metallic thud followed by a few sharp, metallic clangs as the shuttle docks and the docking clamps lock onto the freighter.

Just then, over the speakers, comes Ms. Norata's voice, "Watch your backs over there. I'm reading one human and six Sulari life signs. There are two Sulari close to the airlock, one on the bridge and three in the cargo bay."

Nathan says, "Thank you, Ms. Norata."

Nathan walks to the back of the shuttle and pushes a button on a small panel next to the airlock. The inner door of the airlock opens, and the two men step inside. Once in, the shuttle's inner airlock door closes behind them. The outer air lock doors on both the shuttle and the freighter open and the two men step off the shuttle and onto the freighter.

As the outer doors on both the shuttle and the freighter close behind them, Nathan says to Mr. Black, "Let's activate our shields."

One at a time they say, "Computer, activate shields."

Their suits' computers reply, "Shields activated."

Nathan says to Mr. Black, "Select your Gatling laser."

One at a time they say, "Computer, weapons select, Gatling laser."

Their suits' computers reply, "Gatling laser selected."

Just then, the freighter's inner airlock door slides open. The instant the door opens, the two Sulari in the corridor adjoining the airlock open fire. Several laser blasts impact the shields on their suits. Their suits' computers report that their shield strength drops by two percent with every blast.

The Gatling laser is mounted in the right forearm of their exo-suits, so Nathan and Mr. Black raise their right arms and open fire. Their Gatling lasers have a very high cyclic rate just like the ones mounted in the wings of the police cruiser, which catches the two Sulari off guard, as there are now hundreds of laser blasts flying at them.

Mr. Black hits and kills the first Sulari in the opening barrage, but the second one has taken cover behind the bulkhead where the airlock joins the main corridor. The Sulari thinks he is clever hiding behind the bulkhead, sticking his weapon around the corner to shoot at them, but Nathan has a few tricks up his sleeve. Nathan uses the suit's interactive heads up display to cycle through his available weapons. He finds one he thinks will take care of this problem and selects it by simply looking at it for a few seconds.

He smiles and thinks, "I've got him now."

Nathan puts his hand on Mr. Black's shoulder, so Mr. Black stops firing.

Nathan says, "I've got this."

The weapon Nathan has selected is mounted in the left forearm of his exo-suit, so Nathan takes a step past Mr. Black, raises his left arm and fires. A ball of what looks like liquid blue flame fires from the barrel on Nathan's left arm and streaks towards the bulkhead the Sulari is hiding behind. The ball grows in size as it travels towards the Sulari. When it hits the bulkhead, it instantly liquefies the metal, blowing right through it, striking the Sulari square in the chest. The Sulari's torso, upper arms and his thighs instantly liquefy and splatter green goo all over the corridor walls. The remaining chunks of him fly in all directions and end up spread out all over the floor in the corridor.

Mr. Black looks at Nathan and says, "Holy shit, what was that?"

Nathan looks back at him with a little smile on his face and says, "Plasma cannon."

Mr. Black smiles and says, "Cool."

Nathan and Mr. Black cautiously make their way up to the bridge and enter through what is left of the main doorway. It's charred, twisted and broken like someone tried to shoot their way in, but when that didn't work, they used an explosive charge. As soon as they step onto the bridge a

Sulari opens fire from behind the main navigation station. Nathan and Mr. Black move back into the corridor for cover.

Nathan can't get him with the plasma cannon because it would destroy the navigation station, so he pulls the assault rifle out of the large holster on his right leg. He uses a small joystick that is positioned right where his thumb sits on the pistol grip part of the stock to select a guided projectile with an explosive tip. He changes the scope to infrared and locks on to the Sulari's heat signature. He points the barrel of the rifle into the bridge and pulls the trigger. Instead of a loud bang, that you would normally expect when you fire a rifle, Nathan and Mr. Black here a sharp "whoosh" noise as the projectile is launched. The projectile flies towards the upper front left corner of the bridge, then turns to the right and fires at the Sulari hiding behind the navigation station. The projectile hits the Sulari in the side of the head and then explodes leaving nothing above the neck intact. The Sulari's body slumps to the floor.

Mr. Black says, "Nice shot, Captain."

Nathan smiles and says, "There's nothing like an old school assault rifle shooting guided, explosive tipped solids."

Nathan puts the assault rifle back in its holster and goes over to the captain of the freighter. He's lying on the floor leaning against his chair. He's badly hurt, but he's alive. Nathan can tell by the plasma burns that he's been shot at least three times and estimates he doesn't have long to live.

Nathan kneels down and asks, "What are you carrying that the Sulari would want so badly?"

Struggling to breathe and speak, the captain answers, "I'm not sure really. We're carrying medical supplies, engine parts and a few crates full of rock."

"A few crates of rock? What kind of rock? Where is it from?"

"Three crates of rock from a tiny, out of the way planet called Trynx 3."

Nathan looks up at Mr. Black and says, "More ore from Trynx 3. What the hell is so special about this ore that the Sulari would risk starting a war to get their hands on it?"

Mr. Black says, "I don't know, but we better make sure they don't get their hands on any of it. I've got a bad feeling about this."

"Agreed. So do I."

Nathan turns back to ask the captain where the crates of ore are, but the captain has succumbed to his wounds.

Nathan stands up and says, "Come on Mr. Black, let's head to the cargo hold."

"Aye Captain."

Nathan and Mr. Black cautiously make their way down the corridor to the cargo hold. Before opening the doors, they both select their plasma cannons. Just as Nathan is about to touch the panel to open the cargo hold doors, the doors slide open, and Nathan and Mr. Black find themselves face to face with two Sulari. All four of them are surprised. Mr. Black is the first to react, firing his plasma cannon, at point blank range, into one of the Sulari's abdomens. The Sulari is instantly cut in half, his torso liquefies and splatters green goo everywhere, including all over the front of Mr. Black's exo-suit. The second Sulari panics after seeing this and backs away while raising his weapon towards them. Nathan fires his plasma cannon and cuts the second Sulari in half, splattering green goo everywhere. The last Sulari is hiding amongst a stack of large crates and is taking pot shots at Nathan and Mr. Black. Nathan switches to his Gatling laser and opens fire on the crates cutting them, and the Sulari hiding amongst them, to pieces.

Nathan and Mr. Black take a quick look around to make sure there are no more Sulari hiding in the cargo hold and then they go over and pull up the shipping manifest on the computer console. They find the entries for the three crates that contain the ore from Trynx 3, quickly locate them, and then take them back to the airlock.

Nathan says, "Let's head back up to the bridge. We'll turn on the auto distress beacon so the recovery team can find the ship easily."

"Aye Captain."

Upon entering the bridge, they find the communications console and activate the beacon.

Nathan and Mr. Black head back to the airlock and load the crates on the shuttle.

Once the airlock is secure, Nathan says, "Okay Mr. Bell, take us back to the ship."

"Aye Captain."

Mr. Bell releases the docking clamps and separates the shuttle from the freighter using the maneuvering thrusters. Once clear of the freighter, he engages the sub-light engines. In just a few minutes the shuttle is approaching the rear bay of the police cruiser.

As they get closer, the shuttle's computer's voice says, "Automated landing systems engaged, please release all controls."

The computer slows the shuttle down and aligns it with the rear bay. After a few seconds the shuttle passes through the atmospheric force field and touches down smoothly in the center of the bay. Immediately after the shuttle touches down, the engines power down and the shuttle bay doors close.

The three of them work together to park and secure the shuttle, then they grab the crates containing the ore from Trynx 3, carry them down to the lower bay, and secure them in the armory. Nathan and Mr. Black remove their exo-suits, plug them in to recharge, and then lock the armory up again.

Nathan says, "We'll have to clean the goo off those suits when we get home."

The three of them laugh as they head back up to the bridge.

Upon entering the bridge Nathan says, "Ms. Arnoult, contact Planetary Police headquarters and have them send a recovery team to pick up the freighter and give them the freighter's coordinates. After that, get the police chief for me."

"Aye Captain."

After taking his seat Nathan says, "Mr. Black, put us back on course following the trail of breadcrumbs."

"Aye Captain, course laid in."

"Thank you, Mr. Black."

"Mr. Bell, if you please."

"Aye Captain."

The ship accelerates rapidly and soon the crew sees a bright blue flash of light through the bridge windows as the ship enters FTL.

A few minutes later Mr. Bell says, "Captain, we are on course and traveling at 14 TSL."

"Thank you, Mr. Bell."

Just then Desiree says, "Captain, the recovery team has been dispatched and I have the police chief for you."

"Thank you, Ms. Arnoult. Put him on the main view screen please."

"Aye Captain."

The main view screen activates, and the chief appears, sitting behind his desk in his office at police headquarters.

Nathan stands and says, "Hello, Chief."

"Good day Captain Stone, what do you have to report?"

"We were in pursuit of Haggerty and his crew when we received a distress call from an Earth freighter called the Neptune One. We diverted to assist them and when we got there, we found they had been attacked and boarded by the Sulari. We destroyed the Sulari ship, boarded the freighter, took care of the remaining Sulari and found three crates of ore from Trynx 3 in the cargo hold. We confiscated the ore and locked it in our armory. Sir, I need to know what is so special about this ore and why the Sulari want it so badly that they would risk war for it."

The chief says, "I made some inquiries with friends of mine high up in the military who initially told me that information is classified, but after I explained what is going on out there, they filled me in."

"The ore has some sort of temporal property to it. It emits some sort of frequency that, in the right conditions, could have an effect on time. The scientists working with the ore think they can build a time machine using the ore to break the temporal barrier. Apparently, they are close to having a working prototype."

"My theory is the Sulari found out about the ore and want to steal some to make a time machine of their own. For what purpose we don't know, but we need to make sure they don't get their hands on any of that ore."

Nathan says, "Time travel? Are they crazy? There is nothing more dangerous than time travel. We need to find all the ore that has been removed from Trynx 3 and destroy it, then we should destroy Trynx 3 itself so no more of this ore can be mined."

"I agree and all of that is being discussed at the highest levels of the government. The shipments are being tracked, and the military is dispatching heavily armed recovery teams as we speak. They don't want any of that ore getting into the hands of the Sulari."

"Also, since you are in the middle of it out there, I requested some backup for you from the military. Your backup will rendezvous with you in a day or two."

"Excellent, thank you, Chief. This could get out of hand in a hurry."

"Watch your back, Captain Stone. Good luck and good hunting."

"Thank you, Chief. Stone out."

Nathan pushes a button on the command console on his chair to close the channel and shut down the main view screen.

Nathan says, "Well, now we know why the Sulari want the ore so badly. We'll stay on Haggerty's tail and hopefully he will lead us to the Sulari that hired him."

"Stay sharp people. The Sulari will try to prevent us from interfering, and if they find out we have some of that ore aboard, they will come after us."

Nathan presses a button on the command console on his chair to bring up the tracking hologram once again. He sits down and uses his hands to zoom in on the last five breadcrumbs displayed. Extrapolating a straight line from the last five breadcrumbs Nathan determines they are heading for the Lamayan system.

"Mr. Black, how long until we reach the Lamayan system?"

"Approximately sixteen hours, Captain."

"Very well then, let's go get some sleep. It's been quite a day and I want you all at you best when we get there."

One by one the crew members file out and head to their quarters, leaving the ship's automated systems in charge for the night. Mr. Nagata is the last one on the bridge and just before he leaves, he notices a red flashing light on his console, indicating that the gravity plating is offline in the

captain's quarters again. He smiles, shakes his head, exits
the bridge, and heads for his quarters.

CHAPTER 11 - AMBUSH

The next morning, the crew is awake at 07:00 hours and they all meet in the galley for breakfast. The mood on the ship is positive, as it usually is, and there is a lot of laughing and joking around with each other while they eat.

As usual, Nathan and Desiree are the last ones in the galley for breakfast and the other crew members usually make comments to tease them about their morning lovemaking sessions. Even Mr. Nagata, who is usually pretty quiet and has a fairly dry sense of humor, makes a comment this morning.

With a straight face he says, "Captain, this morning I'm going to check out the twitchy gravity plating in your cabin to see if I can find what's causing it to fail at night when you go to bed and again in the morning before you get up. I'm sure it's getting very frustrating by now."

Nobody expected that from Mr. Nagata. After a few moments of disbelief and silence, everyone has a good laugh over his comment, even Nathan and Desiree.

With a bit of a red face, Nathan clears his throat and says, "I wouldn't worry about it, Mr. Nagata. I'm sure it's fine," which is met with another round of laughter.

When everyone is finished breakfast, they head up to the bridge to check the ship's systems and to verify their course. Nathan also checks to make sure that Haggerty has not changed course.

They have eight hours until they reach the Lamayan system, so they use the time to make sure that all of their equipment is ready, just in case. Nathan and Mr. Black head down to the armory to clean the disgusting remnants of the Sulari off the exo-suits. The rest of the crew run systems checks on the ship, the fighter, the ATV and the shuttle to make sure everything is fully operational. They make sure each vehicle's fuel tanks are full and that their weapons stores are fully stocked. When everything that can be checked is checked and rechecked, the crew gathers back on the bridge.

Ms. Norata checks the tracking hologram and says, "Captain, it appears as if Haggerty's ship has reached the Lamayan system and is orbiting the fourth planet. We will arrive in approximately two hours."

"Thank you, Ms. Norata. Please transfer the tracking hologram to my position."

"Aye Captain."

A few seconds later the tracking hologram appears in front of Nathan. Nathan sits there staring at it for a few minutes trying to formulate a plan. Using the swiping motions, he zooms in so he can see the computer-generated model of Haggerty's ship orbiting the planet.

He touches the holographic planet to bring up its summary. It states that Lamaya 4 is mostly a desert planet with an atmosphere very similar to Earth's, so it can sustain life. It also states that a full survey of the planet has not yet been completed, so not much is known about the planet or its indigenous life forms.

After sitting and thinking a little while longer Nathan says, "Mr. Black, Mr. Bell, I want to surprise Haggerty and his crew. Can you drop us out of FTL and come to a full stop directly behind them? That way we can hit them with a full spread of missiles and take down their major systems before they have a chance to react?"

Mr. Black says, "I think we can do that. I will have the computer start the calculations and run a few simulations to confirm."

Mr. Bell says, "If Mr. Black figures out the course and timing, we should be able to come to a full stop less than a hundred meters away, Captain."

"Excellent, get to work."

After about half an hour Mr. Black says, "Captain, I have entered everything into the navigational computer and run a dozen simulations making small adjustments each time. I have fine-tuned everything to drop us out of FTL and come to a full stop fifty meters astern of Haggerty's ship. I've created a program in the nav computer, and all Mr. Bell has to do is run it, the computer will do the rest."

"Excellent work, Mr. Black."

"Thank you, Captain."

"Mr. Bell, run Mr. Black's program now."

"Aye Captain, Mr. Black's program is running. One hour and twenty minutes to intercept."

"Thank you, Mr. Bell."

The crew spends the next hour and fifteen minutes watching the stars streak by and talking about anything that pops into their heads, including how scientists need to figure out a faster way to travel because it still takes too long to go from one system to another.

At the five-minute mark, a red light flashes on Mr. Black's console accompanied by a series of beeps.

"Five minutes until we drop out of FTL, Captain."

"Thank you, Mr. Black."

"Ms. Norata, shields up in reflective mode. Target their FTL drive and sub-light engines and fire a full spread of missiles the second we drop out of FTL."

"Aye Captain, the shields are up in reflective mode, the targets are locked, and the missiles are ready."

"Thank you, Ms. Norata."

Very soon Mr. Black says, "Approaching the Lamayan system and dropping out of FTL in 5... 4... 3... 2... 1... now."

The computer drops them out of FTL and brings them to a full stop approximately fifty meters astern of Haggerty's ship. The instant the police cruiser comes to a full stop the missiles fire and streak towards their targets. A few seconds later the missiles impact Haggerty's ship and explode taking out the FTL drive and the sub-light engines.

"Ms. Norata, damage assessment."

Ms. Norata scans Haggerty's ship and says, "Their FTL drive and sub-light engines are down, and they have lost main power."

"Thank you, Ms. Norata."

"Ms. Arnoult, open a channel."

"Aye Captain, channel open."

"Marcus Haggerty, this is Captain Nathan Stone of Earth's Planetary Police. Your ship is disabled, surrender and prepare to be boarded."

Suddenly, a red light flashes and a series of beeps comes from her console so Ms. Norata interrupts, "Captain, five ships are approaching our position in FTL."

Two seconds later five Sulari ships drop out of FTL in front of Haggerty's ship and instantly open fire on the police cruiser. Four of the Sulari ships are of the same class as the ones they encountered before, but the fifth ship is much larger. The impact of their large laser cannon blasts shakes the police cruiser violently and sparks are flying around the bridge with every blast.

Nathan yells, "DAMAGE REPORT!"

Ms. Norata says, "Minor damage to secondary systems. Shields are reflecting all blasts but shield strength has dropped to eighty percent. I estimate we have a little over two minutes until we have to switch the shields to inductive mode."

Several of the laser cannon blasts reflect off the police cruiser's shields and hit Haggerty's ship. With their main power offline, their shields are down so they are taking a lot of damage. The force of the laser cannon blasts has now pushed Haggerty's ship out of orbit and it's falling towards the planet. It soon enters the upper atmosphere and begins to glow orange as it falls. The ship is soon a fireball streaking across the sky.

The pummeling from the Sulari ships continues and Nathan says, "Ms. Norata, switch the shields to inductive mode and charge them back up again."

Nathan knows he can't take on the five Sulari ships and win, so he thinks for a few seconds and says, "Ms. Norata, bring the external holo-projectors online and run program Invincible battle group five."

Ms. Norata looks puzzled for a second and then says, "Aye Captain, holo-projectors online now. Running program Invincible battle group five."

Nathan pushes a couple of buttons on the console on his chair, the main view screen activates and switches to the aft view. The crew sees the battle carrier Invincible, accompanied by six heavy cruisers, six light cruisers, and ten destroyers drop out of FTL directly astern of their police cruiser. Immediately after dropping out of FTL, the carrier launches wave after wave of fighters.

At that instant the Sulari ships cease fire, they come about one hundred and eighty degrees and accelerate away rapidly, disappearing in bright blue flashes of light as they enter FTL.

The crew cheers as the Sulari ships vanish.

"Ms. Norata, take the holo-projectors offline."

"Aye Captain, taking holo-projectors offline."

All the ships that just dropped out of FTL to save them disappear. Nathan pushes a button on the console of his chair to deactivate the view screen.

The rest of the crew look at Nathan with a slightly puzzled look on their faces, so Nathan explains, "I programmed a bunch of holographic reinforcement scenarios for times like this where we are badly outnumbered. I gambled that in their haste they wouldn't stop to think to check their sensors, they would just turn tail and run."

Mr. Black says, "Brilliant, Captain."

"Thank you, Mr. Black, but I doubt they'll be fooled for long."

"Let's go find Haggerty. Ms. Norata, can you pin point the crash site?"

Ms. Norata says, "Scanning the surface now, Captain."

A minute later she says, "I found them, Captain. I'm transferring the coordinates to Mr. Black's console."

Mr. Black says, "Coordinates received, plotting a course."

"Mr. Bell, take us down."

"Aye Captain."

The ship turns and banks to port. Lamaya 4 now fills the bridge windows. As they drop into the lower atmosphere, they can see a plume of smoke coming up from the ground miles ahead of them. As they get closer, they can see a skid mark in the sand about a mile long, with small bits of burned debris scattered alongside of it.

Haggerty's crew must have gained some control over the ship and leveled it out for more of a controlled crash landing instead of an all-out crash. When they reach the crash site, they can see that the ship is heavily damaged, but for the most part intact.

"Mr. Bell, let's do a low slow circle of the crash site."

"Aye Captain."

Mr. Bell slows the ship down and banks to port, circling the site. Nathan pushes a button on his command console on his chair to activate the main view screen and display the crash site. The crew can see that the rear ramp is open on the ship and there are two trails of footprints leading out into the sand. After about fifty feet, the trails just stop at two small craters in the sand. Craters that seem to have blood splattered around them.

Nathan says, "Oh, that doesn't look good."

Just then a third man runs out of the back of the ship heading towards a large rocky outcropping. The crew watches him run, but he doesn't make it more than fifty feet before a large creature, that looks like a worm crossed with a dragon, comes up out of the sand directly beneath him and eats him in one bite. The creature looks heavily armored, with thick plate scales, and a large mouth with huge teeth. The creature chews him a few times, swallows him, and then disappears beneath the sand again.

Ms. Arnoult gasps and says, "Oh my God."

Mr. Bell says, "Poor bastard didn't stand a chance, he should have stayed in the ship."

Nathan says, "Mr. Black..."

Mr. Black sighs and says, "I know, let's go get the exo-suits."

"Mr. Bell, you have the con."

"Aye Captain."

Nathan and Mr. Black head down to the lower bay, open up the armory, put the exo-suits on, and power them up. They walk over to the ramp and Nathan whacks the large button on the control panel to open the ramp. The ramp opens, the two men can see the desert and the crash site below them.

Nathan radios the bridge and says, "Mr. Bell, set it down as close to the crash as possible, then dust off and stay on station. We may need a quick pick up."

"Aye Captain."

The ship slows down even more and drops. As the ramp skims the sand the two men step off and walk out from under the ship.

Nathan radios the bridge again and says, "All clear."

The ship lifts off, climbs back up to about one hundred feet and begins a slow circle around the crash site again.

The two men are about fifty feet from the crash site. They start walking towards it trying to be as quiet as possible wearing the heavy exo-suits.

After about ten steps the ground shakes and the two men look at each other as if to say, "OH CRAP!"

Nathan yells, "LOOK OUT!"

He pushes Mr. Black aside and then jumps out of the way. The dragon worm bursts through the sand, barely missing Nathan with its wide-open mouth. About twenty feet of the creature is sticking straight up out of the sand. Nathan and Mr. Black make it back to their feet as the head of the creature slowly descends and curls around to face them. It studies them for a few seconds then opens its mouth wide to roar at them. Nathan and Mr. Black open fire with their Gatling lasers, but the creature's scales are so thick that they don't have any effect except make it angry. The dragon worm raises its head and takes in a large breath. The creature's chest plate swells and glow bright red.

Nathan yells, "OH CRAP, SHIELDS!"

Both men manage to raise their suits' shields just in time, as the dragon worm exhales a huge stream of flame just like the dragons did in children's fairy tales. Luckily the shields protect them from being burned to a crisp. They both shoot at it a second time with the Gatling lasers, but again they do very little against that armor. The creature lunges and snaps at Nathan, who sidesteps the attack. Its tail then comes up out of the sand and knocks Mr. Black flying.

Nathan switches to his plasma cannon and fires at the creature's head several times. It dodges the plasma blasts and tries a vertical attack, coming straight down at Nathan with its mouth wide open. Nathan fires his plasma cannon right into the creature's mouth, at point blank range, which instantly liquefies the creature's head and about ten feet of its body. Blue goo splatters everywhere, including all over Nathan. Luckily, the rest of the creature's body falls to the ground beside Nathan, barely missing him. Nathan wipes the blue goo off his visor so he can see again. He looks around to find Mr. Black and sees that he is all right and getting back up on his feet.

Mr. Black laughs and points at Nathan and says, "Now you know what it's like to get splattered. He got you really good."

Unbeknownst to Nathan and Mr. Black a second dragon worm is stealthily rising out of the sand behind Mr. Black. Nathan is still trying to wipe the blue goo off his visor, so he doesn't spot it until it's a few feet above Mr. Black's head.

Nathan spots the worm just as it was about to lunge down at Mr. Black and he yells, "LOOK OUT!"

Mr. Black turns and steps sideways just as the worm snaps, barely missing him. The worm opens his mouth for a second attack just as Nathan fires his plasma cannon. The plasma blast hits the worm's wide-open mouth instantly liquefying and splattering the worm's head, plus a few feet of its body. Once again, the front of Mr. Black's exo-suit is covered in goo.

Mr. Black stands there stunned for a few seconds. He then wipes the blue goo off his visor, turns to look at Nathan and says in a very sarcastic tone, "Thanks."

Nathan laughs a little and says, "You're welcome."

Nathan and Mr. Black make their way over to the crashed ship. They switch back to their Gatling lasers and walk cautiously up the open rear ramp of the ship. They search the ship, eventually ending up in the cockpit where they find

Haggerty, unconscious in the pilot's chair, bleeding from a head wound. Another man in the copilot's chair is dead, impaled by a steel rod during the crash.

Nathan radios the ship and says, "Mr. Bell, set the ship down, we found Haggerty. He's unconscious so we'll bring him onboard and throw him in a holding cell. Then Mr. Black can check him out."

"Aye Captain."

Nathan undoes Haggerty's seat belt, picks him up by his underarms, and drags him out of the cockpit. Outside the cockpit, Mr. Black picks up Haggerty's legs, and they carry him down the open rear ramp and out of the ship.

Mr. Bell sets the ship down fairly close to the crash site, shuts the engines down, and then runs down to the lower bay to open the ramp. After opening the ramp, he runs down and takes Haggerty's legs from Mr. Black. Nathan and Mr. Bell take Haggerty and put him on the bed in the holding cell while Mr. Black removes his goo covered exo-suit. Once Mr. Black is out of his exo-suit, he grabs a medical kit, enters the holding cell and examines Haggerty.

Mr. Bell and Nathan exit the holding cell and Mr. Bell assists Nathan in removing his rather slimy exo-suit. Mr. Bell gets some blue goo on his hands while helping Nathan out of the exo-suit. He looks at his hands in disgust and tries to flick the goo off to no avail.

Just as Nathan has finished getting out of his exo-suit, Mr. Black comes out of the holding cell, locking the door behind him. He puts the medical kit away and then joins Nathan and Mr. Bell to report his medical findings.

"Haggerty has a couple of cracked ribs, a pretty serious concussion and a few minor cuts and bruises. I've given him a pain killer to keep him comfortable and a mild sedative to help him get some rest. He'll be okay in a few weeks."

"Thank you, Mr. Black. Gentlemen, let's get cleaned up, then head up to the bridge and get off this ball of sand before any more of those dragon worms pop up."

The three men stop at their respective cabins to get cleaned up and then head up to the bridge. Nathan is the last to enter the bridge.

As he enters, he says, "Okay, Mr. Bell, get us off this ball of sand and head for space."

"Aye Captain."

The jet engines fire, and once they have spun up, Mr. Bell pushes the throttles about halfway open. Sand flies and swirls around the ship as it lifts off. The ship finally emerges from the small sandstorm when it reaches about one hundred and fifty feet. Mr. Bell switches from vertical takeoff mode to flight mode and rams the throttles wide open. The ship screams off across the sky, it climbs rapidly, and the sky soon turns black around them as the ship leaves the planet's atmosphere. At this point Mr. Bell disengages the jet engines and closes the air intakes. He then engages the sub-light engines and rams the throttles wide open. The ship accelerates, almost violently, to achieve escape velocity.

The ship's computer announces in its female voice, "Now leaving Lamayan 4's gravity. Artificial gravity plating is coming online."

CHAPTER 12 - FOOL ME ONCE

Just as they break orbit, a series of beeps comes from her console and Ms. Norata says, "Captain, there are five ships dropping out of FTL right in front of us."

Nathan stands up out of his chair and says, "Shields up in reflective mode."

"Aye Captain, shields up in reflective mode."

The same five Sulari ships that Nathan scared off with his holographic simulation drop out of FTL less than one hundred meters away from the police cruiser and they immediately open fire with their large laser cannons. The ship is shaken pretty hard by the impacts, and sparks are flying all over the bridge. They must have figured out Nathan's deception with the holographic fleet and come back for the Trynx 3 ore.

"Mr. Bell, evasive maneuvers."

"Aye Captain."

Mr. Bell banks the ship down and away from the Sulari ships.

"Damage report."

Mr. Nagata says, "Captain, those first shots damaged the FTL drive, all other systems nominal."

"Mr. Nagata, get down to the engine room and see if you can get the FTL drive back online."

Mr. Nagata says, "Aye Captain," then gets up and runs off the bridge.

The Sulari ships pursue the police cruiser around the planet and continue blasting away with their large laser cannons. The shields are reflecting the blasts that Mr. Bell fails to evade, but the cruiser is still taking small amounts of damage from the shaking caused by the impacts. Sparks continue to fly around the bridge with every impact on the shields. After a few minutes the Sulari ships come to a full stop and cease firing.

Desiree says, "Captain, we are being hailed by the Sulari commander."

"Mr. Bell, bring us about one hundred and eighty degrees and come to a full stop."

"Aye Captain."

The police cruiser turns to face the Sulari ships and comes to a full stop about two kilometers away.

"On screen please, Ms. Arnoult."

"Aye Captain."

Captain Creeksto's hideous face appears on screen. He appears surprised to see Nathan.

"Well well well, Admiral Stone, I didn't expect to find you on a police cruiser."

"Hello Creeksto, I've been expecting you to crawl out from the rock you've been hiding under, and it's Captain Stone now. I retired from the EDF."

"Ah yes, Captain Stone, I almost forgot how cocky and smug you are. You have something I want, give it to me and you can leave unharmed."

"And what would that be, Creeksto? Mr. Haggerty?"

"I don't care about Haggerty. He is just a thug I hired to steal what I want. I want the ore from Trynx 3, but you already know that don't you, Captain Stone?"

"Yes, I know what you want, Creeksto, but I don't have any of that ore."

"Don't lie to me, Captain Stone. I know you destroyed one of my ships and confiscated the ore from the Earth freighter."

"Ooooooooh that ore. Well you can't have that ore Creeksto."

"Give me the ore, Captain, or I will kill everyone on board your ship and take the ore. You don't…"

Just then Ms. Norata cuts off the audio and says, "Captain, there are twenty-one EDF ships approaching our position from astern in FTL," and then restores the audio.

Creeksto is still ranting about how they don't stand a chance against his five ships, when Nathan interrupts him.

"Oh, good God, would you shut the hell up already? I'm giving you until the count of five to turn around and get out of here Creeksto."

A little surprised Creeksto says, "Have you gone mad Captain Stone? You are out-numbered and massively out-gunned. Where is your tactical advantage this time?"

Just then one of Creeksto's officers yells, "CAPTAIN, THERE ARE…," but he's too late.

Nathan crosses his arms, smiles and says, "There it is, Creeksto."

Three Invincible class battle carriers, four heavy cruisers, four light cruisers and ten destroyers drop out of FTL behind the police cruiser.

Creeksto says, "Please, Captain Stone, did you really expect me to fall for the same trick twice?"

Turning and taking a seat in his chair Nathan looks at the view screen, smiles, and says, "No, Creeksto, I didn't."

At that moment the battle carriers', the heavy cruisers', and the light cruisers' large laser cannons raise, take aim and unleash hell on the five Sulari ships. All five Sulari ships sustain damage after the first salvo. After the second salvo two of the smaller Sulari ships have taken heavy damage, they are crippled and drifting out of control.

Creeksto is stunned and has a look of shock and disbelief on his face.

"You're out-numbered and massively out-gunned, Creeksto. The way I see it, you have two choices. Turn tail and run or stay and be destroyed."

Creeksto's ship is shaking horribly with the impact of every laser cannon blast, sparks are flying from the bridge systems, lights are flashing, and alarms are sounding. Creeksto cuts off the transmission so the view screen switches to an exterior shot of the Sulari ships. The two crippled ships explode in huge fireballs. The remaining three ships turn and accelerate away at high speed, disappearing in bright blue flashes of light as they enter FTL.

Nathan says, "Somehow I don't think we have seen the last of Creeksto."

Desiree says, "Captain, we are being hailed by the commander of the battle group."

"On screen please, Ms. Arnoult."

"Aye Captain."

Fleet Admiral Daniels appears on the screen standing front and center on the bridge of one of the battle carriers.

Admiral Daniels says, "Captain Stone."

"Fleet Admiral Daniels, it's good to see you and thank you for your assistance. It's nice to see the Invincible's sister ships completed and in action, sir."

"Yes, we just finished our second training run a few days ago. We christened them the Dauntless, the Intrepid, and the Valiant.

"Excellent names for the ships, sir. Admiral, do you think we could hitch a ride back to Earth? Our FTL drive has been damaged."

"Of course, Captain Stone. You and your crew shall be my guests aboard the Valiant. You're cleared to land on the elevator for shuttle bay alpha. You do remember where that is right, Captain?"

Nathan smiles and says, "Oh yes, Admiral I most certainly do."

"Good. You and your crew report to me on the bridge once you've landed."

"See you shortly, Admiral."

"I'm looking forward to it. Daniels out."

"Mr. Bell, you heard the admiral. Head for the Valiant and put her down on the elevator for shuttle bay alpha."

"Aye Captain, just one question."

"What's that, Mr. Bell?"

Mr. Bell swivels his chair around, smiles and says, "Which one is the Valiant?"

Everyone laughs and then Nathan says, "The one in the middle, Mr. Bell, the one in the middle."

Mr. Bell swivels his chair around, fires up the sub-light engines and then nudges the throttles up. He slowly circles the ship around, lines her up, lowers the landing gear, and sets the ship down gently in the center of the massive elevator. After that he shuts down the engines. Ten seconds later, the red strobe lights surrounding the elevator, light up and rotate. The atmospheric force field activates, and the elevator starts to lower the police cruiser into the shuttle bay.

As the tail of the police cruiser clears the flight deck, the huge shuttle bay doors above them begin to close. The crew looks out into the massive shuttle bay and the flurry of activity below them. When the elevator reaches the deck, a tug drives over, hooks up to the nose gear, and tows the police cruiser off the elevator. The tug then turns it around and backs it into one of the repair bays. The ground crew quickly secures the police cruiser to the deck and then the tug disconnects and drives off.

The massive elevator rises back up towards the flight deck, the doors open as it approaches, and it locks in place with a loud metallic thud when it reaches the top.

Nathan gets out of his chair and says, "Okay, everyone, shut everything down and let's go."

The crew all answer with, "Aye Captain."

They get to work shutting all the ship's systems down. When finished, they all get up and follow Nathan down to the lower bay. Nathan opens the ramp and they walk out into the shuttle bay.

Nathan walks over to a Marine corporal that is standing guard in the shuttle bay and says, "Corporal, we have a prisoner in one of the holding cells in the lower bay. Could you have a detail move him to your brig please?"

"Of course, Captain, right away, sir."

"Thank you, Corporal."

The corporal says, "You're welcome, Captain," then he runs off to grab a few more Marines.

"Mr. Nagata, stay here and supervise the repair of the FTL drive."

Mr. Nagata says, "Aye Captain," then walks over to the ground crew chief to speak to him about the repairs.

"The rest of you, come with me."

The crew follows Nathan over to the carrier's internal tram, they board it, and Nathan touches the island on the tram's diagram. The doors close, the tram starts to move and is soon traveling quite quickly. Before too long, the tram slows down as it pulls into the stop for the island. When the tram stops, the doors open, Nathan and his crew step out onto the platform, and walk over to one of the three elevators. They take one of the elevators up to the bridge. The bridge is on level forty-five of the island which is four hundred and fifty feet above the flight deck, so it takes a little while for the elevator to get there. When the elevator stops, the doors open, Nathan and his crew walk out, turn to their left, and approach the large steel and glass doors that secure the command deck. As they approach, the ship's computer scans and identifies each person, grants them access, and opens the large heavy doors.

As they enter the bridge, Admiral Daniels turns to look, and smiles when he sees Nathan. He walks over to the group and shakes Nathan's hand.

"Welcome aboard the Valiant, Captain Stone."

"Thank you very much, Admiral Daniels. Allow me to introduce my crew. This is my communications officer Desiree Arnoult, my tactical officer Aleena Norata, my navigator David Black, my helmsman James Bell, and my chief engineer Hiro Nagata is overseeing the repair of our FTL drive in your shuttle bay.

"A pleasure to meet you all. Take a few minutes to look around the bridge if you'd like. We've made some improvements on the original design. In a few minutes I will have one of the Marines show you to your quarters."

Everyone answers, "Thank you, Admiral," and then they fan out to have a look around.

Nathan takes a quick look around the bridge and then goes over and leans on one of the window frames so he can look out over the huge flight deck. Even though he commanded the Invincible for five years, he is still in awe of the size of the ship.

Desiree walks up from behind him, puts her arms around him and says, "This ship is amazing. It's hard to believe how big it is."

"Yes, she is, isn't she?"

"Do you miss the Invincible?"

Nathan straightens up, puts his arms around her and says, "In some ways I do, yes, but it was time for a change."

Admiral Daniels says, "Okay, Captain Stone, if you and your people will follow the Marine corporal outside, he will show you to your state rooms," gesturing towards the large bridge doors.

The large steel and glass doors open as Nathan and his crew approach them. Nathan steps out and greets the corporal.

The Marine gestures towards the elevators and says, "This way please, Captain Stone."

They take one of the elevators down to level forty, where the state rooms for VIPs are located.

When the doors open, the corporal steps out of the elevator and says, "If you will all follow me please."

He leads them down a wide corridor then turns right into a narrower corridor. He walks about twenty feet, stops at the first door on the left.

"Mr. Black, this is your state room."

Mr. Black says, "Thank you, Corporal," then he goes in and looks around.

The Marine leads them down the corridor, drops Mr. Bell at the next state room, drops Ms. Norata at the one after that, and Nathan at the one after that. Nathan and Desiree go into the state room to look around. Desiree is surprised to see that the rooms are so luxurious considering they are on a warship.

Nathan says, "These rooms are reserved for when they are transporting dignitaries to and from summits on other planets."

They walk into the rather large en suite bathroom and see that it has a large bathtub with massaging jets in it. Nathan looks at Desiree to find she already has a devilish little smile on her face and that look in her eye. He knows what she's thinking.

The two of them walk back out into the state room and the corporal says, "If you'll come with me, ma'am, I'll show you to your state room."

Nathan smiles and says, "That won't be necessary, Corporal, we're together."

The Marine looks at Nathan then at Desiree then back at Nathan as if he's not quite catching on.

Nathan winks at the Marine and it was almost like someone turned on a light switch. The Marine smiles at Nathan, his face turns a little red, embarrassed that he didn't catch on quicker

"Yes sir. Of course, sir."

The corporal turns to leave the room, then turns back around and says, "I almost forgot, the admiral would like you all to join him for dinner at 18:00 hours in his private dining room on level forty-eight."

"Thank you, Corporal."

The corporal says, "You're welcome, sir," then turns and walks out the door which slides closed behind him.

Nathan turns around to find Desiree walking slowly towards the large en suite bathroom. As she walks, she removes her uniform jacket and drops it on the floor. Next, she removes her blouse and drops it on the floor. Her pants fall to the floor just as she reaches the bathroom door, and she steps out of them as she enters the bathroom. She pauses for a second and turns around to look at Nathan. She is dressed only in a very sexy emerald green push-up bra and matching string bikini panties. The emerald green color is a perfect match for her pale skin tone and really sets off the red tones in her auburn hair. Desiree doesn't say a word, she can tell by the look on Nathan's face that she doesn't have to.

She walks into the bathroom and starts the water to fill up the tub. She finds some bubble bath in one of the cabinets and pours it in. When the tub is full Desiree removes her sexy bra and panties and steps into the tub. She starts the jets going and almost instantly there are a ton of bubbles and foam in the tub.

She calls to Nathan, "Get in here already."

Nathan had already started getting undressed before Desiree called to him, so he finishes stripping naked and walks into the bathroom.

He sees Desiree relaxing in the tub in a sea of bubbles. Her eyes light up when she sees Nathan's muscular, naked body. Neither of them says a word, Nathan climbs into the tub with her, grabs her and pulls her to him.

They kiss ravenously and their hands begin to explore each other's bodies. Nathan's hands find Desiree's incredible breasts and he squeezes them gently. Desiree is very eager, so she climbs on top of Nathan, grips his large, erect manhood with her hand and guides him inside of her. Nathan knows when she gets impatient like this, he's in for a wild time and she is not interested in slow and gentle.

CHAPTER 13 - MEANWHILE BACK AT TRYNX 3

Admiral Jameson is sitting in the command chair on the bridge of the Invincible. His battle group has been tasked with quarantining Trynx 3.

The planet has been completely evacuated and his orders are to stop any unauthorized ship from approaching the planet by any means necessary. It's absolutely imperative that Trynx 3 remains completely isolated, and the ore is protected.

In addition to the Invincible, his battle group consists of two smaller escort carriers, twenty heavy cruisers, ten light cruisers, and ten destroyers. He has deployed the cruisers and the destroyers evenly spaced out around the planet at the equator, the two smaller escort carriers over the south pole and the Invincible over the north pole. He has also put up an umbrella of two hundred F-114 Tomcat exo-fighters patrolling the space around Trynx 3 in pairs, nothing can get through this net undetected.

Just then his communications officer says, "Admiral, I have an incoming encrypted transmission from Admiral Hollister."

"On screen."

"Aye sir."

A few seconds later Admiral Hollister appears on the main viewscreen.

Admiral Jameson stands and says, "Admiral Hollister."

"Admiral Jameson, we have reports that the Sulari are massing a large fleet of warships just outside of Earth's space. It appears they will stop at nothing to get their hands on that ore."

"We believe an attack at Trynx 3 is imminent in the next twenty-four hours. We are sending the bulk of our fleet to reinforce your battle group, but they are at least six hours away. We recommend deploying a web of sentry satellites to bolster your defenses until the rest of the fleet arrives."

"Aye sir, the web of satellites will be in place ASAP."

"Good luck, Admiral Jameson. Hollister out."

Admiral Jameson pushes a button on the command console on his chair to close the channel and shut down the main view screen.

"Tactical, you heard the admiral, prepare the sentry satellites for launch and deploy them as soon as they are ready."

"Aye sir. How many satellites do you wish to deploy?"

Admiral Jameson swivels his chair to look at his tactical officer and says, "All of them."

"That's two hundred and fifty satellites, sir."

"Yes, I am well aware of that, mister. You better get busy."

"Aye sir."

His tactical officer gets busy programming the computers to set up the web around the planet. These sentry satellites are floating weapons platforms armed with missiles, powerful laser cannons and defensive shields. The tactical officer just has to program the computer with how he wants the web setup. Then when the satellites are launched from the carrier, they fly to their assigned coordinates around the planet, they deploy their tracking systems and weapons arsenal, and then activate. At that point anything that comes into range, that is not squawking a valid Earth Defense Force transponder code, gets blown out of the sky.

Half an hour later the tactical officer says, "Admiral, I have finished programming the web and I am ready to deploy the satellites."

"Very well, deploy the satellites."

The tactical officer presses a few buttons on his console and says, "Satellites deploying, sir. Estimated time to web completion is forty-five minutes."

"Excellent. Thank you, Tactical."

The sentry satellites are housed in a bay near the bottom of the hull about mid-ship. Two bay doors, one on each side of the ship, slide open revealing five launch tubes per side. The launch system is all automated and can launch ten satellites every sixty seconds. The satellites are ejected from the launch tubes using a high-pressure blast of compressed air. Once they have cleared the hull small control rockets guide the satellites to their assigned coordinates. It takes twenty-five minutes to launch all two hundred and fifty satellites, about another twenty minutes for them to reach their assigned coordinates, and another five minutes to deploy their tracking dishes, missile launchers and laser cannons.

After the last satellite has activated, the tactical officer says, "Admiral, all sentry satellites are in place and active."

"Thank you, Tactical."

"CAG, coordinate with the CAGs on the escort carriers. Let's light up the flight decks and roll out every fighter we have so they are ready to launch at a moment's notice. We could find ourselves in a major battle at any time and I want to be ready."

"Aye sir, lighting up the flight deck now, Admiral."

He types an encoded message to the CAGs on the escort carriers telling them to do the same. They send back messages acknowledging the order.

"Admiral, the CAGs on the escort carriers have acknowledged your order and are lighting up their flight decks as we speak."

There are two force field emitters on the battle carrier that handle "lighting up" the flight deck. One is at the very top of the sensor mast on the island and the other runs around the entire perimeter of the flight deck. When powered up, these emitters glow bright blue and form an incredibly strong force field bubble that encases the flight deck, the upper superstructure and the island. This bubble is then filled with a heated atmosphere, allowing people to work outside on the flight deck, free of the bulky space suits.

When there is no star close by to provide light to see, a large holographic, octagonal light station can be activated. When activated, the light station appears at the top of the force field bubble and is bright enough to light up the entire flight deck so the ground crews can see what they are doing.

Having this force field allows the CAG to utilize the huge flight deck of the carrier to stage all five hundred of his fighters for simultaneous VTOL launch in an emergency situation.

Once the force field bubble has formed and has been filled with the heated atmosphere, the CAG says, "Admiral, the flight deck is lit up."

"Thank you, CAG. Get your fighters on deck. I'm going to step outside."

"Aye sir."

Admiral Jameson walks over to the air lock, opens the inner door and steps in. The inner door closes behind him and then he opens the outer door. This is the first time the flight deck has been lit up since he has taken command of the Invincible, so this will be the first time he has walked outside the ship. He steps out of the air lock, which is to the rear of the bridge, on the port side, and walks around to the front of the bridge, past the windows he normally sits behind every day.

It's a daunting feeling to be walking on the outside of a spaceship, in space, with no space suit on, let alone a spaceship this big.

If you can imagine, standing on what is basically a balcony on the forty-fifth story of a forty-eight story skyscraper, on a ship that is a mile and a half long and two thirds of a mile wide, in space, hovering over a planet, looking out at millions of stars and other celestial bodies, with nothing visible between you and oblivion. This is something that man could only dream about a hundred years ago. You never forget your first time.

Down on the flight deck, the admiral sees the ground crews towing fighters off the elevators and down the deck to the bow of the ship. It will take a couple of hours for the ground crews to fuel, arm, and position the hundreds of fighters along the flight deck. Admiral Jameson spends the next two hours leaning on the railing, enjoying the amazing view.

CHAPTER 14 - BACK ON THE VALIANT

Back on the Valiant, Nathan and Desiree have moved from the tub to the bed, and both of them are panting hard like they just finished a marathon. Nathan is lying beside Desiree with his arms wrapped around her, all of her strength and energy has been drained and her body feels like a big blob of Jell-O.

Desiree says, "Oh my God, what did you do to me?"

Nathan chuckles and says, "I can't tell you, that's a trade secret."

Desiree laughs and tries to squeeze Nathan, but her muscles are completely worn out.

She kisses him on the neck and says, "Oh, I could stay in bed with you forever."

"Me too my love, but we need to get ready for dinner with Admiral Daniels. I better go down to the cruiser and get us some fresh clothes."

Desiree tightens her arms around him to keep him from getting up and says, "No, make love to me again."

"Later sweetheart, we have to get ready for dinner. You rest here for a bit and then get in the shower. I'll be back with our clothes shortly."

Nathan untangles himself from Desiree's arms and gets out of bed. Desiree admires his naked body as he walks over to grab the clothes he left lying on the ground.

Nathan works out a lot and is very muscular. She admires his wide shoulders, his strong back, his trim waistline and his muscular butt that she always jokingly says he could crack a walnut with.

Nathan gets dressed, comes back over to the bed, gives Desiree a quick kiss and says, "I'll be back in a few minutes, Baby."

"You better be."

Nathan smiles at her and then turns and walks towards the door. The door slides open as he approaches and then closes behind him after he walks out into the corridor.

He heads to the elevator and takes it back down to the tram. There is a tram sitting there waiting when he comes out of the elevator, so he walks right on and touches shuttle bay alpha on the tram's diagram. The doors close, the tram begins to move, and is soon traveling quite quickly. Before too long, the tram slows down and pulls into the stop for shuttle bay alpha.

The shuttle bay is a hive of activity, there are hundreds of ground crew personnel working on a number of ships and shuttles including his. There are shuttles taking off and landing, there are shuttles being prep'd for launch and shuttles being parked in bays until they are needed.

Nathan makes his way over to the police cruiser and walks up the open ramp into the lower bay where he finds Mr. Nagata replacing a burned-out relay.

Nathan walks over to him and asks, "How are the repairs coming along, Mr. Nagata?"

"Oh, very well, Captain. The engineers from the Valiant helped me diagnose the FTL drive, and we found the problems in no time. It turned out to be a few burned-out relays, and a fried control sensor. We replaced the damaged components and ran the diagnostics. The FTL drive is fully operational again."

"Excellent work, Mr. Nagata. So, are you all finished in here then?"

"Yes, Captain, I just finished replacing one of the ramp relays."

"Very well, I'm going to grab a few things and then I'll show you to your state room. We're all having dinner with the admiral at 18:00 hours so get cleaned up."

"Very well, Captain, I'll get changed and meet you back here in about ten minutes."

Nathan nods at Mr. Nagata and then heads to his quarters where he grabs a complete change of uniforms for Desiree and himself. When he goes into Desiree's lingerie drawer, he has trouble deciding what to take because she has so many sexy things to wear. He finally decides on a black and pink bra and panty set. He throws the lingerie into a bag along with her makeup kit and hair products. When Nathan has everything they need, he heads back down to the lower bay where he finds Mr. Nagata has already changed and cleaned up and is waiting for him.

"Follow me, Mr. Nagata."

"Aye Captain."

The two men walk down the ramp out of the ship and into the shuttle bay. They head over to the tram and take it back to the carrier's island stop. They take the elevator up to level forty and make their way down the corridor to their state rooms.

Nathan shows Mr. Nagata to his state room and says, "See you in the admiral's private dining room on level forty-eight at 18:00 hours."

Mr. Nagata says, "Very well, Captain," and then goes into his state room to look around.

Nathan goes back into his state room and sees that Desiree is no longer in the bed, so he opens the bathroom door to find her in the shower. He quickly hangs up the uniforms in the closet and drops the bag on the floor outside the bathroom.

He stands there watching Desiree in the shower for a bit and thinks, "Oh my God, she's so sexy and beautiful, I'm so lucky."

He watches her wash her hair and soap up her sexy body, especially enjoying the part when she soaps up her incredible breasts. Suddenly, he realizes that he has to have her, and he has to have her now. He quickly strips off all his clothes and walks over to the steamy hot shower. He quickly opens the door, steps in, grabs her around the waist with his left hand, and clamps his right hand over her mouth so she can't scream from being surprised.

Desiree is very surprised and a little scared because she doesn't know who just grabbed her in the shower. She's really hoping it's Nathan. She quickly recognizes the feel of his body pressed up against hers and relaxes.

He steps forward and presses her against the glass wall of the shower, he drops his hand from her waist and picks up her left leg, pulling it out to the side.

Desiree's hands come up to the glass wall to brace for what's about to happen.

Nathan enters her swiftly from behind with almost brutal force, and Desiree screams into the hand that is clamped over her mouth. Nathan is overcome with raw animalistic lust and takes her as hard, as fast, and as rough as he can. He removes his hand from her mouth, grabs her hair and pulls it which causes her head to turn and tilt exposing her neck. He bites her hard on the neck causing her to yelp in between her moans.

It doesn't take either of them long to reach orgasm with the intensity and force of Nathan's thrusting.

Panting, Desiree says, "What got into you? You were such an animal, I loved it."

"Just seeing your sexy naked body in the shower all soaped up, GRRRRRRRRR, BABY!!!"

Desiree smiles and says, "OOOOOOH, BABY."

The two lovers finish showering, dry off and go into the bedroom to get dressed. Nathan hands Desiree the bag he packed from the cruiser. She pulls out the lingerie that Nathan chose for her to wear.

She looks at Nathan with a devilish grin on her face and says, "Mmmmm good choice, Baby, these are damn sexy. Are you going to be thinking about what I'm wearing under my uniform when we are having dinner with the admiral?"

Nathan smiles and says, "Hell yeah I will be. I'll be thinking about the lingerie and what's in the lingerie."

Desiree smiles and says, "You're so bad."

She then turns and walks back into the bathroom to get ready.

"I'll be ready in thirty minutes."

"Perfect."

Nathan gets dressed then sits down to relax for a bit and before he knows it, Desiree is shaking him to wake him up.

"Nathan, wake up, it's time to go to dinner with the admiral."

Nathan wakes a little confused as to where he is and what time it is.

"Okay, wow I must have nodded off. I guess you really wore me out."

Desiree giggles and says, "Come on we're going to be late."

She pulls Nathan off the couch and they walk out of their state room and down the corridor to the elevators.

They take the elevator up to level forty-eight and find the admiral's private dining room. The rest of Nathan's crew are already there enjoying cocktails and hors d'oeuvres before dinner is served.

The battle group has jumped into FTL and Nathan's crew are watching the stars streak by through the huge windows in the dining room, which is located atop the island just above the bridge. It's a truly amazing view.

Admiral Daniels joins them shortly after Nathan and Desiree come in. He pours himself a scotch, holds it up for a toast and says, "Welcome, everyone."

Nathan says, "Thank you for having us, Admiral."

Admiral Daniels says, "A short while ago we received a message from Admiral Hollister. He said that the Sulari are massing a large fleet of warships just outside Earth's space, and it's believed that an all-out attack on Trynx 3 is imminent."

"He has ordered the bulk of Earth's fleet to Trynx 3 and ordered us to rendezvous with the fleet as soon as possible. We are to set up a defensive blockade and stop any Sulari ships from landing on Trynx 3 by any means necessary."

"Under no circumstances is any of that ore to fall into Sulari hands. We should arrive at Trynx 3 about the same time the rest of the fleet arrives, in about six hours."

Nathan says, "I'm afraid I don't know a lot about the Sulari, I've only had the two run-ins with Captain Creeksto. What all do we know about them?"

Admiral Daniels says, "Well we know they are an arrogant, aggressive race, who thinks they are a far superior species to all others. They don't respect other species' borders and are constantly causing intergalactic incidents by getting caught trying to sneak into their neighbor's space. They want to conquer and rule the known galaxy but lack the technology, and quite frankly the intelligence, to make it happen. They are also known for rash decisions and rushing in without thinking things through, which is mostly due to their over inflated egos."

Nathan says, "That certainly describes Captain Creeksto, that's for sure."

Admiral Daniels says, "We can easily anticipate and out think them, and our technology is far superior to theirs. I don't think they have actually developed any of their technology themselves. It's all been bought or stolen from other species."

"We suspect the Sulari are working with another species to develop a time machine, because quite frankly they're not smart enough to develop one themselves. If successful, they could go back in time and destroy or conquer any species that currently stand in their way, back in the past. This is why it's imperative that we do not allow even a single gram of that ore to fall into the Sulari's hands."

Nathan says, "Absolutely, Admiral."

The chef comes out of the kitchen and says, "Ladies and gentlemen if you would all please take your seats, dinner will be served momentarily. Thank you," then he walks back into the kitchen.

Everyone sits down at the dinner table with Admiral Daniels at the head of the table, Nathan, Desiree and Ms. Norata to his right. Mr. Bell, Mr. Black, and Mr. Nagata take seats on the admiral's left. The table is set formally with stemmed water glasses, white and red wine glasses, fine china and beautifully polished silverware.

Immediately after everyone has taken their seats, seven porters come out of the kitchen carrying dinner plates with polished silver domes over top of them. When all seven plates have been set in front of the admiral and his guests, the porters lift the domes off simultaneously, revealing their meals.

The entrée tonight is steak Oscar, lobster tail with melted lemon cilantro butter, grilled asparagus and scalloped potatoes.

The porters file back into the kitchen and the chef returns to check on everything.

The admiral says, "Everything looks delicious, Chef. Thank you very much."

Nathan and his crew join in praising the chef for preparing such a delicious meal for them.

The chef says, "Thank you so very much and I hope everyone enjoys their food. Please let one of us know if you need anything else," and then walks back into the kitchen.

One porter comes back into the dining room with two bottles of wine. Starting with the admiral he asks, "Would you care for some wine with your dinner, sir?"

Admiral Daniels says, "Yes please, I will have the white."

The porter pours the admiral a glass of the white wine and then continues around the table. When everyone has been poured a glass of wine, the porter retreats to the kitchen once again.

The group spends the next hour enjoying their meals, drinking wine, and laughing at anecdotes shared by the admiral and Nathan about "the good old days".

When they are all finished their meals, the chef serves them crème brûlée for dessert. Nathan and Desiree like to eat fairly healthy, so they politely turn down the decadent dessert when it's offered to them by one of the porters.

Nathan leans over and whispers in Desiree's ear, "I'm going to have you for dessert when I get you back to the state room and strip you down to your sexy lingerie."

Desiree blushes a little and then whispers in Nathan's ear, "You promise?"

Nathan just smiles back at her.

When everyone is done eating, Nathan says to his crew, "We should probably turn in early and get a good night's sleep. We could have a very big day tomorrow and I want everyone alert and well rested."

His crew all respond with, "Aye Captain," and stand up from the table.

Admiral Daniels stands up as well and each crew member shakes his hand and thanks him for dinner before exiting the dining room.

Nathan is the last to shake his hand, "Thank you very much for dinner, Admiral, and have a pleasant evening."

Nathan's crew is waiting for him by the elevators. They all ride down together and say goodnight to each other before going into their respective state rooms.

Nathan goes into the bathroom to brush his teeth and get undressed for bed. When he comes out, he finds Desiree lying across the bed in a very seductive pose wearing only her sexy lingerie. Nathan knows, by the look on her face, what she wants.

He walks over to the bed drinking in her sexy body with his eyes. He crawls over to her on all fours and she rolls over onto her back as he crawls on top of her. He looks into her beautiful eyes and then lowers his head to kiss her. They kiss passionately, their mouths making love, their excitement building quickly. Nathan brings his hands up and squeezes her breasts through her bra. His fingers find the clasp on the front of the bra and pop it open. He pushes the bra cups to the side revealing her perfect breasts, his hands cupping and squeezing them gently.

Desiree lets out a little moan, enjoying the attention from Nathan's hands.

Nathan breaks their kiss and begins kissing Desiree's neck, each kiss a little lower than the last, he kisses her collar bone, he kisses the upper part of her chest and works his way down in between her breasts. He kisses his way across her left breast, finds her nipple, and sucks on it.

Desiree puts her hands on the back of his head and lets out a soft moan letting Nathan know she loves what he's doing.

He takes his time, sucking gently, switching back-and-forth, kissing and sucking on both breasts. After a few minutes Nathan kisses down her stomach towards her sexy little panties. When he reaches her panties, Desiree spreads her legs. He kisses her through the panties a few times and then pulls them to the side with his hand.

Desiree inhales sharply when Nathan's mouth and tongue touch her. Desiree's hands find the back of Nathan's head and she pulls his hair and moans loudly as he pleasures her.

Nathan can tell her excitement is building very quickly as her hips begin to thrust, Nathan wraps his arms around her thighs to control her movements.

Moments later her breathing changes and she screams out in pleasure as she reaches a powerful climax.

Nathan lifts his head and smiles as he watches her writhe in pleasure.

He crawls his way back up her body, kisses her on the cheek and says, "Oooooh, Baby, that was incredible."

Panting and barely able to speak Desiree says, "It sure was."

Nathan says, "If you liked that, you're going to love this."

Desiree smiles up at Nathan, she feels his hand pull her little panties to the side and feels the tip of Nathan's large erect manhood touch her.

Nathan lowers his head to kiss Desiree as he slowly enters her.

She moans into his mouth until he is all the way inside her.

Nathan stays completely still, making love to Desiree's mouth with his until neither of them can stand it. Nathan starts to thrust in and out of her, very slowly and gently, while continuing to kiss like only they do. Soon their excitement is building, and their pace is increasing. Both of them moan as their climax is building. It doesn't take very long at all before they are both overtaken by intense orgasms.

When the two lovers recover, they shift positions and lie on their sides with Nathan behind Desiree. Nathan wraps his arms around her and holds her tight as they both drift off to sleep with smiles on their faces.

CHAPTER 15 - GUARDING TRYNX 3

Nathan wakes the next morning and rolls over to see the clock on the nightstand says 07:00 hours.

He thinks to himself, "We could have a very big day today, so we better get up and get moving."

He rolls over to find Desiree still sound asleep with a very peaceful look on her face. She is so beautiful he takes a minute to just stare at her.

He thinks to himself, "I'm so lucky."

She is sleeping so soundly that he hates to wake her up, but they need to get moving.

He puts his hand on her shoulder and whispers, "Des, wake up, it's 07:00 hours so we need to get moving," but she only stirs a little and whispers something incoherent.

He tries again this time shaking her gently and speaking a little louder, but she only moves her head from side to side.

He smiles and thinks to himself, "I know what will wake you up."

He climbs on top of her and kisses her passionately. Within just a few seconds her lips start to kiss him back, her arms wrap around him and her beautiful eyes flutter open.

Nathan breaks the kiss, pulls back and says, "Good morning my love. It's about time you woke up, we need to get up and get moving."

Desiree whines and says with a pouting expression on her face, "No I don't want to get up, I want to stay in bed with you all day."

Nathan says, "Sorry, Baby, we can't. We have to be ready in case the Sulari show up," and then he tries to get out of bed.

Desiree pounces on him and says, "Oh no you don't."

Nathan and Desiree wrestle on the bed for a few seconds and then Nathan stands up, picks her up, and throws her over his shoulder. He walks into the bathroom and right into the shower with her laughing, kicking, and screaming. He turns the water on and then sets her down under the stream of nice hot water. He soaps up her sexy body, paying extra attention to her incredible breasts.

Desiree says, "Oh, I could get used to this kind of treatment."

Nathan smiles at her and says, "Wash your hair, we need to get going."

Nathan is finished his morning routine before Desiree, so he takes a few minutes to look out the windows of their state room. He sees a reddish-brown planet to starboard, which he assumes is Trynx 3. At first glance, it appears to be nothing more than a lifeless hunk of rock in space. There are no visible signs of water or plants from orbit, it seems to be very similar, in many ways, to Mars back home in their solar system. Just off the port bow he sees a very large purple ringed planet with a small moon orbiting it. Beyond that he sees a beautiful pink and purple nebula with a dense cluster of stars at its center.

When Desiree is ready, the two head down to the mess hall for breakfast. When they walk in, they find the rest of their crew just sitting down to eat. Nathan and Desiree join the lineup for food, and both select a large serving of bacon and eggs, toast, fruit, coffee and orange juice. They walk over and join their crew at their table. They say good morning to everyone and sit down to eat. Desiree sits down beside Ms. Norata and Nathan sits across from them.

Ms. Norata smiles when she sees how much food Desiree and Nathan have on their plates.

She leans over and whispers teasingly in Desiree's ear, "Worked up quite the appetite last night, did we?"

Desiree giggles and nudges Ms. Norata in the side with her elbow, which is returned in short order by Ms. Norata.

Nathan notices the two of them giggling, elbowing each other, and blushing, so he knows it's one of those unspoken conversations about sex. Nathan just chuckles, shakes his head and continues to eat.

The crew engages in small talk while they eat, discussing the food, how weird it is to be back on board a battle carrier, and how the Sulari will get their butts kicked if they dare to show up and challenge the fleet.

When everyone has finished eating Nathan stands and says, "Admiral Daniels would like to see us on the bridge after breakfast."

They all answer, "Aye Captain," and then stand up to go.

Everyone walks out of the mess hall and down the corridor to the elevators. They take an elevator up to the bridge level, then exit the elevator and walk towards bridge doors. Just as before, the computer recognizes Nathan and his crew and automatically opens the large, thick, glass and steel doors allowing them access to the bridge.

As Nathan and his crew walk onto the bridge Admiral Daniels turns and says, "Good morning, everyone, I hope you slept well."

Nathan and his crew answer almost in perfect unison, "Yes, Admiral, thank you, sir."

The admiral smiles at Nathan as if to say, "You can take the man out of the military, but you can't take the military out of the man."

Nathan smiles back in acknowledgement and asks, "Has the whole fleet arrived, Admiral?"

Admiral Daniels says, "Almost, Captain Stone. We left a few escort carriers and light cruisers at home to watch over the Earth."

"Our battle group arrived at almost the precise moment the battle group arrived from Earth. This is the first time that we have had a fleet this size together in the history of the Earth Defense Force. This is also the first time all four of our battle carriers have been together."

"We have close to three hundred and twenty ships and a few thousand fighters forming a defensive line that the Sulari will have to break through. If any of them break through, the web of sentry satellites will take them out. The Sulari don't have a snowball's chance in hell of getting through to Trynx 3."

Nathan says, "Very impressive, Admiral."

"By the way, Captain Stone, the flight deck is lit up if you and your people would like to step outside."

The other crew members all look at each other and smile.

Desiree, being the only one who hasn't served aboard a battle carrier, says, "Excuse me? Step outside?"

Nathan laughs and says, "When we say that the flight deck is lit up, we mean there is a force field covering the top section of the carrier that holds in a heated atmosphere. This allows us to work out on the flight deck and to go outside on the walkways of the island without the encumbrance of a space suit."

"If you look out at the edge of the flight deck, you can see a bright blue force field emitter that runs around the entire perimeter of the deck. There is also another emitter at the top of the island. The two emitters work together to form an incredibly strong force field."

"The system also has multiple redundancies to ensure the force field stays up, no matter what, to protect the lives of the people working outside."

Nathan and his crew take a couple of steps towards the airlock to the rear of the bridge, but Desiree doesn't move. She just stands there looking apprehensive.

"What about things like solar radiation?"

Nathan comes back over to her, puts his hand on her upper arm and says, "Sweetheart it's totally safe. Believe me, we have all done it. The force field stops all radiation from the star."

"You're sure it's safe?"

"Yes, it's perfectly safe. I understand it's a little daunting, the first time always is. Walking outside a spaceship, in space, with no spacesuit on goes against everything we have ever seen or have been told but believe me it's perfectly safe and well worth it."

Desiree reluctantly nods her head in agreement, so Nathan takes her by the hand and walks her over to the airlock. Nathan opens the inner door of the airlock, they all step inside, and then the door closes behind them. Nathan opens the outer door of the airlock. He looks at Desiree and nods his head. She nods back and they step out of the airlock together.

Nathan says, "See, you're perfectly fine."

Desiree answers with a simple, "Uh-huh," and squeezes his hand tighter.

They all walk forward until they reach the front of the island on the port side, overlooking the flight deck. Desiree grabs the railing, which is a little higher than average, and grips it tight.

She looks down over the side and says with a great deal of fear in her voice, "Oh my God, I never realized we were so high up."

Nathan puts his arms around her and says, "Baby, looking down forty-five stories to the flight deck is nothing. The real show starts when you look up."

Desiree doesn't move for a few seconds, then she slowly lifts her head and looks up and what she sees is amazing.

Stars, millions and millions of stars. She sees Trynx3, the nearby ringed planet, the nebula, the other three huge battle carriers, the rest of the fleet, and the vastness of space.

Desiree is not normally left speechless, but all she can manage to say is, "Wow."

Nathan giggles, kisses her on the cheek and says, "You never forget your first time."

The crew spends about an hour walking around outside the bridge. They stare at the stars, the planets, the fleet and the nebula. They also watch the ground crews on the flight deck lining up hundreds of fighters so they are ready to take off at a moment's notice should the Sulari show up.

Sitting around waiting for something to happen is no fun but looking at an amazing view like this is a great way to pass the time.

Nathan and his crew head back inside for a status update.

Upon reentering the bridge Nathan asks, "Anything yet Admiral?"

"Nothing yet, Captain Stone, it's all quiet out there."

"I wonder what they're waiting for. Do you think they detected our fleet and changed their minds?"

The admiral turns to look at Nathan and says, "It's possible I guess, but the Sulari want that ore so badly I doubt they would just give up that easily."

"I guess all we can do is wait."

Admiral Daniels turns back to looking out the front bridge windows and says, "Yes indeed, Captain Stone, yes indeed."

Nathan decides there's not much he and his crew can do on the bridge and he doesn't want to be in the way, so he says to his crew, "Come on everyone, let's go to the recreation area and find something to do while we wait."

Several hours pass by and still no Sulari fleet. Nathan and his crew watch two movies and play a bunch of games in the recreation area to pass the time.

Suddenly, at 16:00 hours the battle stations alarm sounds and over the ship's address system comes, "Battle stations, battle stations, all hands man your battle stations, this is not a drill, I repeat this is not a drill."

Nathan jumps to his feet and says, "Okay, everyone, let's head to the bridge and see what's happening."

The crew jumps to their feet and the six of them run down the corridor to the elevator. They head up to the bridge level and walk onto the bridge to find it bustling with activity.

Nathan sees that Admiral Daniels is busy giving orders, but something is not quite right. He doesn't see any Sulari ships through the bridge windows, there are no laser cannon blasts flying by, and the fighters on the flight deck are just sitting there, they're not launching.

Suddenly, the battle carrier leans hard to port and initiates an emergency turn.

Nathan looks out the port bridge windows at the rest of the fleet and sees two more battle carriers, half of the heavy cruisers, light cruisers and destroyers are turning with the Valiant.

As soon as the battle group has formed up, they all engage their FTL drives and accelerate rapidly away from Trynx3. Seconds later a bright blue flash of light comes through the bridge windows as they enter FTL.

Nathan says, "Something must have happened, let's go find out what's going on."

Nathan and his crew walk over to Admiral Daniels and Nathan asks, "What's happened, Admiral?"

Admiral Daniels turns to look at Nathan and says with a very grave look on his face, "At precisely 16:00 hours we received a distress call from Earth stating they are under attack."

"From what we can ascertain, what we believe to be the entire Sulari fleet dropped out of FTL just outside Earth's defense perimeter and immediately opened fire on the ships we left there to guard the planet."

"Our ships were taken completely by surprise and were destroyed almost immediately. Next, they took out the sentry satellites. Then they did something very peculiar, they just stopped."

"Earth is defenseless with an enemy fleet numbering in the neighborhood of a hundred and seventy-five ships hovering over the planet and we are six hours away."

Nathan and his crew are stunned and don't know what to say. Fear and a feeling of helplessness overtakes everyone.

Just then the Valiant's communications officer says, "Admiral, I have the video feed coming through now."

Admiral Daniels says, "On screen."

"Aye sir."

Admiral Daniels says to Nathan and his crew, "This is video footage from the sentry satellites before they were destroyed."

The video footage shows the Sulari fleet drop out of FTL almost right on top of the two escort carriers and the six light cruisers left to defend Earth. The Sulari opened fire the instant they appear and destroy all eight ships within just a few minutes. It then shows the Sulari starting to destroy the sentry satellites, the video feed cutting off and showing static as they destroy the last satellite.

The bridge is deathly silent except for the hum from the equipment and the beeps from buttons being pushed.

Just then the communications officer says, "Admiral I have another message coming in from Earth. It appears to be a video feed from one of the far Earth orbit telescopes. It must have been turned around to face the planet."

Admiral Daniels says, "On screen."

"Aye sir."

The video feed shows a huge dog fight going on between the Earth and the Sulari fleet. Hundreds of fighters from both sides are swarming around and laser cannon blasts are flying in every direction. After a few minutes the entire Sulari fleet opens up with their smaller laser cannons and soon destroys all of Earth's fighters.

A few minutes after the last of Earth's fighters is destroyed, one of the Sulari ships begins to move. The telescope follows the ship and zooms in on it. The Sulari ship enters into a high orbit and comes to a full stop.

Nathan says, "What the hell are they doing?"

Admiral Daniels says, "I have no idea, but I have a really bad feeling about this."

After a few minutes, the video feed shows what looks like a shuttle bay door open on the side of the Sulari ship. Two small ships fly out of the shuttle bay towing an unknown device with their tractor beams.

Nathan says, "What the hell is that?"

Admiral Daniels says, "I don't know."

The small ships tow the device a few kilometers away from the Sulari ship and then come to a full stop. The small ships then turn off their tractor beams and return to the Sulari ship, leaving the device sitting in space.

Whoever is controlling the telescope zooms it out to view the Earth, the moon and the Sulari fleet.

A few minutes later, hundreds of missiles launch from the Earth's surface and from the military base on the moon. All of the missiles are converging on the device.

The Sulari send their fighters in to destroy the missiles and protect the device. Hundreds of Sulari fighters blast away at the missiles and manage to shoot down most of them. A few of the Sulari pilots sacrificed themselves to save the device by crashing their fighters into the missiles when they couldn't hit the missiles with their laser cannons. The remaining fighters withdraw and land back aboard their mother ships.

Next, all of the Sulari ships, except the one that deployed the device, turn and move off out of the view of the telescope. The telescope zooms back in on the remaining ship and the device.

The device just sits there for a few minutes and then suddenly unfolds what look like two black solar panels. At the center of the device, a cylinder-shaped casing splits in thirds lengthways and opens. The pieces of the casing pivot out of the way on hinges, exposing a thick walled silver drum that's outer surface is covered with a web of small devices. The silver drum spins, and five thin rings light up a bright neon blue inside its hollow center core. The drum spins faster and faster until it's just a blur. When it reaches its maximum rotational speed, several red lights on the body of the device begin to blink. Starting out slowly at first then increasing their rate.

At this point the Sulari ship that deployed the device turns and moves off in the same direction the rest of the Sulari fleet went earlier.

After a few minutes, the blinking red lights on the body of the device suddenly turn solid red.

Ten seconds later, the communications officer says, "Admiral, I am receiving an emergency transmission from Earth."

The Admiral says, "Split the screen. Put the device on one side and put the incoming transmission on the other."

"Aye sir."

The incoming transmission shows a large, computerized, control room that is shaking violently, and pieces of the ceiling and walls are falling everywhere.

A captain in an Earth Defense Force uniform, that is unknown to Admiral Daniels, steps into the camera's view and says, "Admiral, the entire planet is experiencing massive earthquakes and as a result, massive tsunamis are forming in every ocean. We are evacuating the government and the military leaders," then the transmission cuts off.

The transmission from the telescope again takes up the entire view screen. The telescope zooms out to show the Earth, the device and the moon.

Nathan says, "Oh my God, are the Earth and the moon getting closer together?"

Admiral Daniels says, "My God, I think you're right."

Nathan says, "That thing must be an artificial gravity well generator."

Admiral Daniels says, "Son of a bitch, they're going to crash the moon into the Earth."

Nathan says, "That will kill everything on Earth almost instantly."

The noise level on the bridge goes up exponentially as the bridge crew panic over what they are seeing. The Earth and the moon move towards each other with greater speed and all they can do is watch helplessly. Within just a matter of seconds the moon slams into the surface of the Earth.

Some of the bridge crew cry and scream out as they watch their planet being destroyed.

The force of the impact splinters half of the moon and about a third of the Earth. A few seconds later there is a huge explosion, ejecting large chunks of both out into space. When the explosion clears enough that the telescope can see the planet again, the bridge crew sees what remains of the Earth. A third of the planet is gone, and the core is exposed to space. There is a massive red ribbon of fire traveling outwards from the impact crater, encircling the planet, burning off the atmosphere and flash boiling the oceans into vapor. In less than a minute, the Earth and everything on it, is dead. The surface of the planet is covered with lava and black scorched earth.

Everyone on the bridge is devastated, many of them weeping uncontrollably and crying out.

Admiral Daniels is sitting down in his chair holding his head in his hands.

Nathan is fighting back tears while holding Desiree, who is sobbing on his chest.

Mr. Black has tears running down his face while holding Ms. Norata, who is crying uncontrollably.

Mr. Bell and Mr. Nagata are half sitting, half leaning on a computer console, legs straight, their arms crossed, one hand on their foreheads hiding their faces.

The next five hours are the longest hours of their lives.

When the battle group arrives at what used to be their home, they enter orbit around what's left of the Earth. The flight decks of the battle carriers and the escort carriers are still lit up so almost everyone on the carriers are lining the flight decks and the external walkways on the islands to see the devastation and destruction firsthand.

The moon has been destroyed and the remnants have been ejected out into space by the force of the explosion. A third of the planet is gone, the core is exposed, and molten lava is flowing freely around inside the crater and across some of the planet's surface. The rest of the planet is black, charred ground. Several volcanoes can be seen throwing red, glowing lava high above the surface.

The mood among the crew is a mixture of sadness and anger, with most of the crew calling for the admiral to hunt down the Sulari fleet and wipe them out.

The question on everyone's mind is, what do we do now?

Do we go out into space and find an uninhabited world similar to Earth and start over?

Do we ask for refugee status on the home world of one of our neighbors?

What do we do?

Admiral Daniels is leaning on the railing outside the bridge surveying the devastation. After one full orbit he says, "Okay, everyone, back to your stations."

The bridge crew files back inside through the airlock and takes their positions. When the communications officer sits down at his console, he sees a light flashing and his console is beeping in time with the light indicating that they have an incoming transmission.

He puts his headset back on and pushes a button on his console. Through his headset he hears, "Attention EDF battle carrier Valiant, Admiral Daniels do you copy?"

The communications officer pushes a button on his headset and says, "This is the EDF battle carrier Valiant, one minute for Admiral Daniels."

The communications officer stands up and says, "Admiral Daniels, I have an incoming transmission for you."

Admiral Daniels says, "On screen."

"Aye sir."

The Secretary of the Fleet, Admiral Hollister appears on screen. He appears to be standing in a large control room.

Admiral Hollister says, "Admiral Daniels, if you have finished your survey of the planet, I would like you to bring your battle group to Mars. I'm sending your navigator the coordinates. I'll expect you shortly. Hollister out."

The main viewscreen powers off and Admiral Daniels and Nathan look at each other, puzzled as to what's going on.

Both of them wondering, "Why would we go to Mars? There's not much there."

Admiral Daniels says, "Comms, alert the fleet and send them the coordinates sent by Admiral Hollister."

"Aye sir."

"Navigator, set course for Mars."

"Aye sir, course laid in.

"Helm, engage the FTL drive and take us to Mars. Speed 1 TSL."

"Aye sir, engaging the FTL drive now. Speed 1 TSL."

The huge battle carrier, along with the rest of the battle group, accelerates rapidly away from what is left of the Earth. A few seconds later there is a bright blue flash of light through the bridge windows as the ship enters FTL.

It's a short trip to Mars, just a mere twelve minutes at the speed of light, so it's not long before the helmsman drops the ship out of FTL and comes to a full stop at the provided coordinates. Mars now fills the windows of the battle carrier's bridge.

The communications officer says, "Admiral, I have an incoming transmission, audio only."

Admiral Daniels says, "Let's hear it."

The voice that comes over the speakers is Admiral Hollister's, "Admiral Daniels, welcome to Mars, if you would be so kind as to jump in a shuttle and come on over. Oh, and bring Captain Stone along with you."

Admiral Daniels says, "Yes, Admiral Hollister. Just one question. Where are we going?"

Just then a huge space station, that appears to be twice the size of a battle carrier, decloaks right in front of the Valiant and her battle group.

Then Admiral Hollister says, "I'll meet you in shuttle bay two. That's the big door right in front of you with the big number two painted on it. Hollister out."

Admiral Daniels turns to Nathan and says, "Captain Stone, if you would come with me please."

Nathan says, "Of course, Admiral."

Nathan turns to his crew and says, "Stay here, I'll be back soon."

The crew all respond, "Aye Captain."

The two men exit the bridge through the large glass and steel doors and take the elevator down to the tram level.

Admiral Daniels asks Nathan, "Did you know anything about this secret base?"

Nathan says, "No sir, I had no clue it even existed. It's as much of a surprise to me as it is to you."

When the elevator doors open, Nathan and the admiral walk over to the tram and take it to shuttle bay alpha. When the tram arrives in the shuttle bay, they walk over to the first shuttle in line in the bay. They climb aboard, Nathan takes the pilot's chair, and the admiral takes the copilot's chair.

Nathan puts on a headset and activates the comm system, "Valiant air traffic control, this is Captain Stone requesting clearance for takeoff from shuttle bay alpha, port side."

"Captain Stone, this is Valiant air traffic control, clearance granted, no traffic in the immediate area, have a safe flight."

"Thank you, Valiant air traffic control. Lifting off."

Nathan pushes the throttles up a little and the shuttle lifts off the deck. He turns it ninety degrees to port and nudges it forward towards the huge shuttle bay doors. A few seconds later the shuttle passes through the atmospheric force field and out into space.

It's a very short flight to the shuttle bay on the space station. As their shuttle approaches the doors, a few rotating orange warning lights illuminate and spin. A few seconds later the doors begin to open. The doors are large and slow, but eventually disappear into the floor and the roof of the shuttle bay. Nathan brings the shuttle in, spins it around one hundred and eighty degrees, and sets it down gently on the deck. He then powers down the shuttle and opens the door. The Admiral and Nathan exit the shuttle and are met by Admiral Hollister.

Admiral Hollister shakes both their hands and says, "Gentlemen, welcome to Mars Station X-Ray."

CHAPTER 16 - IN THE NICK OF TIME

Admiral Daniels asks, "Admiral Hollister, what is this facility?"

Nathan says, "Yes, what is this place? I've never even heard a whisper of its existence."

"This is an ultra-top-secret research and development lab, designed and built to develop and test new weapons and new technology away from the population of Earth in case something was to go wrong. It also allows us to keep the weapons and tech we are developing a secret. What better way to develop tech that doesn't exist, but in a lab that doesn't exist? Its existence was kept on a strictly need to know basis. Captain Stone, those Gen 4 exo-suits I sent you were developed, and tested, right here."

"Thank you for those by the way, they have come in handy a few times."

"You're welcome, but if you like those, you're going to love what I'm about to show you. Follow me, gentlemen."

The admiral turns and walks towards the door. Nathan and Admiral Daniels follow Admiral Hollister out of the shuttle bay and down a short corridor to an elevator which they take to level five of the facility.

When the doors open, they walk down another short corridor to a door guarded by two well-armed Marines.

As the three men approach them, the Marines snap to attention and salute both of the admirals.

Admiral Hollister returns their salute, then scans his key card through a slot in the security panel beside the door. After that he punches in his key code and finally moves his face close to the panel for a retinal scan of his right eye. The doors slide open and the three men walk into what appears to be a research lab with about a dozen scientists, in white lab coats, working around a machine in the center of the lab.

Admiral Hollister turns to them and says, "Gentlemen, our scientists have developed and tested a time machine, powered by the ore that is mined on Trynx 3. The very ore that the Sulari would love to get their grubby little flippers on."

"We have run several limited scale tests, sending inanimate objects and lab rats back and forward in time an hour or two with great success. Now we will use it to save the Earth from destruction. All we need is more power. The kind of power produced by the reactors of a battle carrier."

"We are going to recall the rest of the fleet from Trynx 3, connect the time machine to the reactors and shield emitters of the Valiant, and send the fleet back in time twenty-four hours to stop the Sulari from destroying the Earth."

Nathan and Admiral Daniels say nothing, they are just looking at Admiral Hollister with blank stares, unsure if he is pulling their legs or not.

"Don't believe me? I assure you I am deadly serious. Admiral Daniels, if you would please recall the rest of the fleet from Trynx 3."

"Aye sir."

"Captain Stone, I would like you to use your tactical genius to come up with a sure-fire plan to stop the gravity well device from being deployed and of course wipe out the Sulari fleet. I don't want a single Sulari ship to survive the battle. We're going to send the Sulari a message. Understood?"

"Understood, Admiral."

"Excellent. Get to it gentlemen."

Admiral Daniels salutes Admiral Hollister and says, "Aye sir."

Nathan and Admiral Daniels make their way back down to the shuttle bay, board their shuttle, take their seats and close the door. Neither man has said a word to the other. They are still trying to process what they have just learned. To say they are both a little skeptical would be an understatement.

Nathan puts on a headset and activates the comm system, "Mars Station X-Ray air traffic control, this is Captain Stone requesting clearance for takeoff from shuttle bay two."

"Captain Stone, this is Mars Station X-Ray air traffic control, clearance granted, no traffic in the immediate area."

"Thank you, Mars Station. Lifting off."

Nathan pushes the throttles up a little and the shuttle lifts off the deck. He nudges it forward towards the shuttle bay doors and a few seconds later the shuttle passes through the atmospheric force field and out into space. As soon as he clears the station, he heads straight for the Valiant, which is just a few kilometers away.

As they approach the battle carrier, Nathan activates the comm system once again, "Valiant air traffic control, this is Captain Stone requesting clearance to land in shuttle bay alpha."

"Captain Stone, this is Valiant air traffic control, you are cleared to land in shuttle bay alpha, port side."

"Thank you, Valiant air traffic control."

Nathan lines the shuttle up with shuttle bay alpha from the port side. He slows the shuttle as he nears the carrier and is soon passing through the atmospheric force field and into the bay. With a metallic clang, Nathan sets the shuttle down on the deck, powers it down, and opens the door.

The two men exit the shuttle and head off across the shuttle bay to the carrier's internal tram. They take the tram to the island station and then take an elevator up to the bridge. When the elevator stops, the doors open, the two men step out and turn to the left. As they approach the bridge, the ship's computer identifies them and automatically opens the two large, thick, glass and steel doors that secure the command deck of the ship.

As they step onto the bridge, the ship's computer announces in its female voice, "Admiral on deck," and everyone stands and snaps to attention.

Admiral Daniels says, "At ease everyone," then the bridge crew take their seats again.

The admiral walks over and stands beside his command station, leaving Nathan standing just inside the bridge doors.

"Comms, get me Admiral Jameson aboard the Invincible."

"Aye sir."

A minute later the communications officer says, "Admiral, I have Admiral Jameson for you, sir."

"On screen."

"Aye sir."

Admiral Jameson appears on the main view screen.

He salutes and says, "Admiral Daniels."

"Admiral Jameson, I'm recalling the fleet. Rendezvous with my battle group at Mars. You are to get under way immediately, we have a mission to complete."

Admiral Jameson salutes and says "Yes sir, we'll be under way shortly. Jameson out."

The main view screen powers down and goes blank.

Nathan's crew gathers around him and Desiree asks, "Captain, what's happening? Why are they recalling the fleet to Mars?"

"We have a plan, a plan that if it works, could save the Earth from being destroyed."

Mr. Black says, "But the Earth has already been destroyed, unless…"

Mr. Bell says, "Unless they have a working time machine."

Nathan smiles, but says nothing.

Desiree asks, "They have a time machine? A working time machine?"

Nathan says, "Yes, it's being transferred to the Valiant as we speak. Admiral Hollister promises it will work, and he wants me to come up with the tactical plan to stop the Sulari from deploying the gravity well device and destroying the Earth."

"I'm going back to my state room to work. I want the rest of you to head back down to the shuttle bay and go through our ship from stem to stern and make sure she is ready for action."

They all answer in unison, "Aye Captain."

Desiree kisses Nathan and then they all head down to their ship.

Nathan heads down to his state room to work on the tactical plan. Upon entering the state room, he heads right for the office and accesses the Valiant's network through the computer console built into the desk. He pulls up the satellite video feeds for the time period from when the Sulari drop out of FTL until they slam the moon into the Earth. He makes notes of key points in time, the distance between the Sulari fleet and Earth when they drop out of FTL, and their approach vector. He also makes note of which ship is carrying the gravity well device, the exact moment it drops out of FTL, and its precise coordinates. He transfers all this data into a hologram that shows the Earth, the moon, the Sulari ships, the second they drop out of FTL, and the position of the satellites that captured the video footage. He now has a very accurate baseline model to use to plan his attack.

Next, he has the computer add models for every ship in the EDF fleet, and then he sits back and contemplates where to position the ships. He starts with the battle carriers and works his way down to the smaller ships. He even factors in how to place the ships so he can bring the maximum number of their huge laser cannons to bear on the enemy ships. He decides the fleet should be cloaked, lying in wait for the Sulari ships to drop out of FTL, guarantying the element of surprise.

Next, Nathan assigns each ship in the fleet a Sulari target. The odds will be better than two to one for the EDF. As he works out the small details, he realizes that even with the element of surprise, their superior weapons and superior numbers, there is still a possibility of losing several ships in an all-out battle with the Sulari fleet.

After a few hours of planning, analyzing and running simulations he feels he has a solid plan, and that Earth is safe from being destroyed, but he has been unable to come up with a way to reduce the number of casualties projected. To Nathan, losing one ship is one too many. As the hours pass, he is getting frustrated, so he takes a break and grab a big glass of ice water. As he is walking from the office to the bar, he passes a mirror hanging on the wall.

Suddenly it hits him, "We have an insurance policy."

He laughs out loud looking at his reflection in the mirror and high fives himself. He is now satisfied with his plan and takes it up to the bridge to share it with the Admiral Daniels. Then if Admiral Daniels approves it, they will share it with Admiral Hollister. When Nathan gets back up to the bridge, he sees that Admiral Hollister has shuttled over from the space station.

He says to himself, "Okay, change of plan. I guess I will present my plan to both of them at the same time."

Nathan walks over to the admirals and says, "Admiral Hollister, Admiral Daniels, I have a plan I wish to present for your approval."

Admiral Hollister says, "Excellent, Captain Stone. Admiral Daniels, may we use your office to go over Captain Stone's plan?"

"Of course, Admiral this way," and motions towards a door at the back of the bridge.

The three men go into Admiral Daniels' office and Nathan presents his plan using the hologram he put together in his state room.

At the conclusion of Nathan's presentation, Admiral Hollister shakes Nathan's hand and says, "Brilliant, absolutely brilliant, Captain Stone."

Admiral Daniels says, "I agree, Captain Stone. You came up with a brilliant plan that saves the Earth, maximizes their casualties and minimizes ours."

Nathan says, "Thank you, thank you both. How is the installation of the time travel device coming along?"

Admiral Hollister says, "The scientists have it installed in the engineering section and are hooking it up to the reactors and the shield emitters as we speak."

"Once that's done, they will run some tests and simulations on it so they can calculate how much power to feed the time machine to create a time bubble big enough to encompass the entire fleet. We should be ready to go in a few hours when the rest of the fleet gets here."

Nathan says, "Excellent. With your permission I will distribute my plan to the commanding officers of every ship in the fleet and then I will head down to my ship to see if my crew has her ready for battle."

Admiral Hollister says, "Very well, Captain Stone."

Nathan transmits the plan to all the commanding officers in the fleet, then leaves the admiral's office, exits the bridge, and heads to the elevator. He takes the elevator down to the tram level and then takes the tram to shuttle bay alpha.

He walks over to his ship and up the ramp into the lower bay. He makes his way up to the bridge where he finds his crew still checking systems and running diagnostics, double and even triple checking the systems to make sure the ship is ready.

A few hours later, the rest of the fleet arrives from Trynx 3. The scientists have finished installing, testing and calibrating the power for the time machine and they have installed the control console on the bridge.

Before leaving the bridge, the lead scientist goes over to Admiral Daniels and Admiral Hollister and says, "We were able to make a time bubble with a fifteen kilometer diameter. You have to get all the ships in the fleet within seven point five kilometers from the center of the Valiant. Anything outside the bubble will be severed and left behind. The control console will tell you if everything is inside the bubble's radius before you activate the time machine."

Admiral Daniels says, "Understood, thank you."

The lead scientist says, "You're welcome and good luck, Admiral. My team and I will be in the engineering section monitoring the time machine should you need anything," and then he exits the bridge through the large glass and steel doors.

Admiral Daniels says, "Helm, move us one hundred kilometers away from the station out into open space and come to a full stop."

"Aye sir."

"Comms, send a message to the commanding officer of every ship in the fleet. Tell them to form up on the Valiant and that they have to be well within a seven point five kilometer radius from the center of the Valiant. It's going to get very crowded around here so tell them to use their thrusters and to move slowly and carefully so we don't have any collisions."

"Aye sir."

A few seconds later the sub-light engines ignite, and the massive battle carrier turns and moves away from the space station out into open space. When it clears one hundred kilometers, the helmsman brings the ship to a full stop.

"Admiral, we are one hundred kilometers out and the helm is showing all stop."

"Very well, thank you, Helm."

It's at this point that Nathan and his crew enter the bridge through the big glass and steel doors, not wanting to miss a second of watching the fleet perform these extremely close quarters maneuvers.

Soon other ships from the fleet arrive and begin moving into close formation with the Valiant. The other three battle carriers position themselves immediately around the Valiant. The Dauntless is positioned on the starboard side, the Intrepid on the port side and the Invincible directly above the Valiant. Never before have these ships been so close to one and other. You could almost step from one flight deck to the other they are so close.

Nathan and his crew are standing at the port side bridge windows watching nervously as these massive ships slip together as close as they can.

Once the battle carriers are all tucked in tight, the escort carriers surround them and slip in as close as possible, followed by the heavy cruisers, the light cruisers, and finally the destroyers. When the last ship has maneuvered into place, it looks like a massive steel ball fifteen kilometers across floating in space. They have tucked just about three hundred war ships inside the specified spherical diameter. The fleet is now ready to jump back in time.

Admiral Daniels walks over to the control console for the time machine and powers it on. He follows the instructions the lead scientist gave him and checks to make sure that every part of every ship will be inside the time bubble. The system gives him a green light, indicating that every ship will be inside the bubble when it forms. Next, he sets the date and time to jump back to into the control console. Once he has set that, all that's left to do is press the execute button.

"Comms, give me an open channel to the fleet."

"Aye sir, channel open."

"Attention all commands, this is Admiral Daniels. We are ready to execute the time jump. This will be the first time in history that a human experiences time travel, so we don't know what to expect. Prepare yourselves for anything, keep calm and good luck. Daniels out."

Admiral Daniels pushes the execute button. The reactors' power output levels climb as the device forms the large time bubble around the fleet. The display on the control console shows a graphic of the bubble forming around the fleet and a power monitoring graph which is climbing quickly towards one hundred percent.

When the graph reaches ninety-five percent, Admiral Daniels says, "Brace yourselves we're about to jump."

The graph hits one hundred percent, there is a momentary flash of bright white light and then the power levels drop quickly to zero as the bubble collapses.

Admiral Daniels says, "Did it work? Did we jump back in time?"

Nathan says, "Check our position relative to Mars and the space station. We should be approximately one solar day away if it worked."

Admiral Daniels says, "Yes, of course. Navigator, check our distance from Mars."

The navigator checks his console and reports, "We are approximately one solar day away from Mars and there is no sign of the space station, sir."

"Thank you, Navigator."

"Tactical, can you verify that the Earth and the moon are intact?"

The tactical officer performs a scan and reports, "Yes sir, they are intact as are the ships we have in orbit."

Admiral Daniels and Nathan smile at each other.

Admiral Daniels says, "Comms, send a message to the commanding officers of every ship in the fleet. Tell them to disperse and set course for Earth."

"Aye sir."

The communications officer sends the message and soon ships on the outer edge of the ball begin to peel off and spread out. It takes about half an hour for all the ships in the fleet to disperse. The last ones to separate are the battle carriers as they were at the center of the ball of ships.

Nathan and his crew watch from the port bridge windows as the Intrepid rolls slightly to port as it turns and pulls away from the Valiant. It's impressive to see this huge battle carrier maneuver from this close.

After a minute or two more, the communications officer says, "Admiral, all commands report they have dispersed and have set course for Earth."

"Thank you, Comms."

"Helm, set course for Earth."

"Aye sir, course laid in."

"Engage the FTL drive and take us home. Speed 1 TSL."

"Aye sir, engaging the FTL drive now. Speed 1 TSL."

The ship accelerates rapidly and soon the crew sees the bright blue flash of light through the bridge windows as they enter FTL. The rest of the fleet engages their FTL drives as soon as they see the Valiant accelerate away. A little more than twelve minutes later, everyone on the bridge sees a bright blue flash of light through the windows as the helmsman drops the ship out of FTL and brings her to a full stop. A few seconds after that, the rest of the fleet arrives in a whole series of bright blue flashes of light.

The Earth fills the windows of the bridge and everyone is happy and relieved to see their home safe and sound. That bright blue ball in space still intact with billions still alive on the surface and its moon still orbiting as it has for millions of years. Also, in view is the small battle group left to defend Earth.

Admiral Daniels says, "Comms, send a message to the CO of that battle group. Tell him there will be a Sulari fleet arriving in about six hours and I want him to pull his ships back close to the planet and that he is to take out anything that gets past us."

"Aye sir."

A minute or two later the communications officer says, "Admiral, the message has been received and acknowledged, sir."

"Thank you, Comms."

From the bridge windows they see the small battle group move off, getting closer to the planet.

After a few minutes, Admiral Daniels looks at Nathan and nods his head.

Nathan jumps to it and executes his plan. First, he goes over to the communications officer, hands him a tablet and says, "Send this as an encrypted message please."

The communications officer takes the tablet and reads the message that Nathan wants him to send.

He looks up at Nathan in disbelief and asks, "Are you sure about this, sir?"

Nathan smiles and says, "Yes, just send it."

The communications officer raises his eyebrows momentarily and says, "Okay sir, sending it now."

A few minutes later the communications officer looks at Nathan a little bewildered and says, "Captain Stone, the message has been received and acknowledged."

Nathan says, "Excellent, thank you Comms. Now open a channel to the fleet."

"Aye sir, channel open."

Nathan says, "Attention all commands, this is Captain Nathan Stone. It's time to execute our plan. Proceed to your assigned coordinates and position your ships as I have specified, sound battle stations, and bring your laser cannons to bear. Stone out."

Ship by ship the fleet moves into position all in accordance to Nathan's battle plan. The Valiant is the last ship to move into place and come to a full stop.

Admiral Daniels says, "XO, sound battle stations."

"Aye sir."

The XO grabs the microphone and announces over the ship's address system, "Battle stations, battle stations, all hands man your battle stations, this is not a drill."

An alarm sounds after his address and the lights on the bridge change from white to red.

After a minute he says, "Admiral, all sections report battle stations manned and ready."

"Thank you, XO."

Nathan walks over to Admiral Daniels, shakes his hand and says, "My crew and I will take our ship out now, Admiral. Good luck, sir."

"Thank you, Captain Stone. Good luck to you and your crew as well."

Nathan turns and walks over to his crew who are still standing by the port bridge windows.

"Okay, everyone, let's gather our things and get back to our ship."

The six of them exit the bridge through the large glass and steel doors and head back to their state rooms to pack up their belongings. When packed, they meet by the elevators and head down to the tram level. From there they catch a tram to shuttle bay alpha. They step off the tram and walk across the shuttle bay to their ship.

Nathan stops and shakes the ground crew chief's hand and says, "Thanks for fixing her up for us, Chief."

The chief says, "You're very welcome, sir and good luck out there."

"Thanks, Chief."

Nathan walks up the ramp into the lower bay, goes to his cabin and drops his things off before heading up to the bridge. When he gets to the bridge, he finds everyone else already at their stations.

Nathan sits down in his chair and says, "Are we ready for this?"

His crew all answer in unison with a resounding, "Aye Captain."

Nathan smiles and says, "All right then let's do this."

"Ms. Arnoult, contact Valiant's air traffic control and request clearance for takeoff."

"Aye Captain."

A minute later Desiree says, "Captain, Valiant air traffic control has granted us clearance for takeoff from the port side bay door."

"Thank you, Ms. Arnoult."

"Mr. Bell?"

Mr. Bell says, "Yes, Captain?"

"Time to try a rolling takeoff. Do you think you can handle it having never tried it in this ship?"

Mr. Bell smiles and says, "Absolutely, Captain."

The sub-light engines power up. When they are online, Mr. Bell pushes the throttles forward slightly and taxis the ship over to the launch area in front of the port side shuttle bay door. When he has the ship in position for launch, a blast shield rises out of the shuttle bay deck to the rear of their ship. When the blast shield is fully deployed, a green light on the bulkhead in front of them lights up, indicating that they can launch when ready.

Mr. Bell rams the throttles wide open, and the ship accelerates rapidly, blasting through the open shuttle bay door and out into space. Mr. Bell pushes the button to raise the landing gear and then banks the ship to port and climbs. He circles the ship around behind the fleet leveling off about two kilometers above the Valiant and comes to a full stop about a kilometer astern of the massive battle carrier. From this position Nathan can see everything and direct the battle according to his plan, just like the quarter back in a football game.

"Captain, we have reached the specified coordinates and have come to a full stop."

"Thank you, Mr. Bell. Was that fun?"

Mr. Bell smiles and says, "Yes, yes it was, Captain."

"Ms. Arnoult, open a channel to the fleet."

"Aye Captain, channel open."

"Attention all commands, this is Captain Nathan Stone speaking. All ships are now in position. Engage your cloaking devices. Stone out."

One by one the ships in the fleet engage their cloaking devices and vanish from view.

When all the other ships have disappeared Nathan says, "Ms. Norata, cloak the ship and bring the shields and weapons online please."

"Aye Captain, cloaking the ship and bringing the shields and weapons online now."

"Excellent, now we wait."

For a little over six hours they wait. They pass the time going over Nathan's plan, they watch a movie, talk about all kinds of things like what's the first thing they will do when they get back home, the most embarrassing moments in their lives, and moments they didn't think they would live through.

Finally, Ms. Norata says, "Captain, the Sulari fleet is approaching in FTL."

Nathan says, "Okay, here we go. You all know what you have to do so get ready."

The Sulari fleet drops out of FTL and comes to a full stop just as they did before. At the instant the Sulari fleet appears, every ship in the Earth fleet opens fire with every large laser cannon that could be brought to bear. Their target is the Sulari ship carrying the artificial gravity well device. Literally thousands of laser cannon blasts impact on the shields of that one Sulari ship, but its shields don't last for long under such an intense barrage. In a matter of ten seconds its shields are down, and the ship is being chewed to pieces by the Earth fleet's big guns. Ten seconds after its shields are down, the ship explodes in a massive fire ball.

The Sulari are surprised and stunned. Since the Earth fleet is still cloaked, they are scrambling to figure out what just happened and where all those laser cannon blasts came from. Their latest intelligence says the Earth fleet is still sitting at Trynx 3.

On the bridge of the Valiant, Admiral Daniels says, "Comms, open a channel to the fleet."

"Aye sir, channel open."

"Attention all commands, this is Admiral Daniels on the Valiant. You all have your assigned targets outlined in Captain Stone's plan, now disengage your cloaks and take them out. Not one Sulari ship leaves here today. That will make them think twice about challenging us again. Daniels out."

Each ship in the Earth fleet disengages their cloak, targets a Sulari ship and opens fire with its large laser cannons.

The Sulari respond by opening fire with their own laser cannons, but the Sulari's laser cannons are not as powerful as the Earth fleet's. Their ships are not as big as the Earth fleet's and their shields are not as strong as the Earth fleet's. Even though the two fleets are going toe to toe exchanging fire, the Sulari are massively outnumbered and out-gunned. It's just a matter of time.

Adding to the all-out assault with their laser cannons, the Earth fleet launches missiles, thousands of missiles.

Though damage is being inflicted by both sides, most of the damage is being taken by the Sulari fleet. The Sulari realize this and start launching fighters to bolster their attack.

The Earth fleet responds by launching their own fighters. The flight decks of the battle carriers and the escort carriers were lit up and lined with fighters ready for takeoff.

The fighters from each side rush out to meet each other in the middle of the battle, dodging laser cannon blasts and missiles. When they reach each other, so begins the largest dog fight in history, with literally thousands upon thousands of fighters involved.

As soon as the Earth fighters get near the Sulari fighters, they open up with their Gatling lasers, blasting many Sulari fighters to bits with their high cyclic rate. The Sulari fighters open up with their smaller laser cannons and take out a few of Earth's fighters, but just like their larger ships, the Sulari fighters are no match for the Earth fighters.

It also seems that Earth's pilots are much better trained than the Sulari's pilots. Everywhere you look in the dog fight there are two of Earth's fighters, the primary and his wingman, chasing one Sulari fighter. They work as a team, quickly destroy the Sulari fighter they are chasing and move on to the next one.

Nathan's ship is still sitting cloaked, above the fleet, watching the battle unfold. Nathan looks across the battlefield and notices one Sulari ship has pulled back from the firing line and climbed above the other Sulari ships, possibly directing the battle on their side.

"Ms. Norata, scan the Sulari ship that has pulled back. Can you tell me if that is Creeksto's ship?"

"One moment, Captain."

Ms. Norata scans the ship and compares it to her scans from their previous encounters with Creeksto's ship.

"Captain, my scans confirm, that's Creeksto's ship. It's identical to the ship we encountered in the Lamayan system. It's the Croixa."

"Thank you, Ms. Norata."

"Mr. Bell, do you think you can slip us around the battle and put us directly in front of that ship?"

"Absolutely, Captain. How close do you want to get?"

"Think you can put our nose five meters away from his bridge windows?"

"That's pretty close, Captain."

"Can you do it?"

"Of course I can, Captain."

"Very well, Mr. Bell, take us in."

"Ms. Norata, how about we cook up something special for our old friend Creeksto? Ready the nano emitters."

Ms. Norata smiles and says, "Aye Captain."

Mr. Bell swings the ship wide around the battle and then lines the police cruiser up in front of the Sulari ship. He slows the cruiser right down to a crawl and comes to a full stop with the nose of the ship five meters away from Creeksto's bridge windows. Nathan and his crew are literally looking their enemy in the face.

"Great job, Mr. Bell."

"Thank you, Captain."

Nathan and his crew can see Creeksto pacing back and forth on his bridge, throwing his arms up in anger and frustration and though they cannot hear him, they can tell he is yelling at the top of his lungs.

"Ms. Arnoult, open a channel, audio only."

"Aye sir, channel open."

Nathan smirks and says, "I see you Creeksto, can you see me?"

Creeksto stops pacing and yelling. He walks up to the bridge windows and looks around. Puzzled, he says, "Stone? Is that you Stone?"

"Yes, it's me Creeksto. You look stressed... and fat. Have you put on weight?"

Creeksto looks puzzled and then looks down at his body to see if he looks heavier. It's then he realizes Stone is looking at him, not looking at his ship, looking at him. Creeksto slowly raises his head and looks out his bridge windows.

Nathan turns and nods at Ms. Norata who in turn shuts down the ship's cloak.

Creeksto's eyes open wide when he sees the nose of Nathan's police cruiser sitting five meters away from his bridge windows.

Nathan is standing with his arms crossed in the police cruiser's front bridge window looking directly at him. The red and blue police lights are flashing and Creeksto can see all the different weapons that are aimed right at him.

Creeksto throws his command tablet across the bridge and yells, "YOU SON OF A BITCH! HOW DID YOU DO IT STONE? HOW DID YOU KNOW? HOW DID YOU GET HERE? OUR SCOUTS REPORTED YOUR FLEET WAS STILL AT TRYNX 3 LESS THAN SIX HOURS AGO!"

Nathan says, "Yeah well, let's just say that we figured out how to be in two places at once."

Puzzled, Creeksto says, "Wormhole? Space folding?"

He pauses for a few seconds and then a look of realization washes over his ugly face.

"You did it didn't you? You broke the time barrier."

Nathan still standing there with his arms crossed says, "I saw what you did Creeksto. Slamming the moon into the Earth with an artificial gravity well generator. Even though we've already foiled your plan, I can't let that go. You know that right?"

"You may have stopped me this time Stone, but I will never give up until your kind are wiped from existence."

Nathan smirks and says, "I was hoping you would say that Creeksto."

"Ms. Norata, if you please."

"My pleasure, Captain."

A few seconds later the bridge windows on Creeksto's ship crack in thousands of places.

Creeksto and the other Sulari on the bridge look puzzled. When they realize what's about to happen, the looks on their faces turn to looks of terror.

Nathan says, "Nano-bots, effective little buggers, aren't they? They can be programmed to attack and destroy anything. Like windows on the bridge of a ship for example."

Before any of the Sulari on the bridge can react, the bridge windows explode outwards into space. Creeksto gets sucked out into space and bounces off the nose of the police cruiser before drifting off into open space. The rest of the bridge crew gets sucked out into space as well, leaving the ship with nobody at the controls.

Following their programming, the nano-bots then turn their attention to the ship's systems and take main power offline. The Sulari ship's shields and weapons are now offline. The ship is dead in space and defenseless.

Nathan returns to his chair and says, "Mr. Bell, back us off five hundred meters."

"Aye Captain, backing away."

When they reach about five hundred meters Nathan says, "Ms. Norata, fire a full spread of missiles into their bridge."

"Aye Captain, firing missiles now."

Four missiles scream away from the wings of the police cruiser and fly into the exposed bridge, exploding on impact. The missiles cause massive damage and set off a series of secondary explosions.

"Ms. Norata, reengage the cloaking device."

"Aye Captain, cloaking device reengaging."

"Thank you, Ms. Norata."

"Mr. Bell, slip us around the battle back to our over watch position behind our fleet."

"Aye Captain, reversing course back to our over watch position."

The police cruiser banks to the right and moves away from Creeksto's ship.

As they move off, the secondary explosions continue to rip through the Sulari ship until they reach the main reactor. The reactor explodes in a massive fireball, engulfing the entire ship. When the fireball dissipates, the Sulari ship is gone, there doesn't seem to be a single remnant of debris left.

When they get back to their over watch position, Nathan and his crew see that the Earth fleet is inflicting major damage to the Sulari fleet while taking very little damage itself.

After a few minutes Nathan notices that several Sulari fighters have broken away from the dog fight and are headed towards the battle carriers.

Nathan stands up out of his chair and says, "Ms. Norata, destroy those fighters before they can get to the battle carriers."

"Aye Captain, targeting the fighters now."

Targeting cross hairs appear around each Sulari fighter on screen.

The retractable missile turrets on the fuselage of the police cruiser deploy and spin rapidly. When they are up to speed, they rapidly fire their miniature missiles at a rate of about four missiles per second. They launch about twenty missiles at each fighter. These missiles are fast and close the gap quickly. The Sulari fighters try to dodge the mini missiles but are unsuccessful. The missiles slam into the fighters in rapid succession, blowing them out of the sky.

Two more fighters break through the battle lines and head directly for Nathan's cloaked police cruiser. They must have seen the missiles emerge from the cloak and triangulated the position of Nathan's ship.

"Ms. Norata…"

Without answering Nathan, she targets the two fighters with the Gatling lasers mounted in the leading edge of the wings and opens fire. The powerful Gatling lasers, with their incredibly high cyclic rate, cut the two Sulari fighters in half before they explode and vanish.

Just then Desiree says, "Captain, I have a message from the communications officer on the Valiant. He says your insurance policy has just arrived?"

Nathan smiles and pushes a button on the command console on his chair to redirecting the main view screen to show the port side. At that exact moment, a second complete Earth fleet drops out of FTL on a ninety-degree vector to the battle. The instant the fleet drops out of FTL, it opens up on the Sulari fleet with every large laser cannon that can be brought to bear, it launches missiles and the carriers launch fighters.

Nathan's crew turn and look at Nathan for an explanation.

Nathan says, "I figured out that if we were successful in traveling back in time, there would be two complete Earth fleets in this time period. The fleet guarding Trynx 3 and the fleet guarding Earth."

"As soon as we arrived at Earth, I had the communications officer on the Valiant contact the Nathan Stone at Trynx 3 and explain everything."

"It took a little convincing, but we got them here. We had a perfectly good fleet sitting at Trynx 3 so why not bring them into the fight for a little extra insurance?"

Mr. Black says, "That's brilliant, Captain."

"Thank you, Mr. Black."

Nathan looks around the bridge of the police cruiser and sees his whole crew smiling in agreement.

The tide of the battle quickly turns now that the Sulari are out-gunned more than four to one. Soon Sulari ships start exploding all across the battlefield. After about five minutes, the whole Sulari fleet is gone. There is nothing left except a lot of floating debris.

The Earth fighters are chasing down the last of the Sulari fighters making short work of them with their Gatling lasers. Once the Sulari fighters are all gone, the Earth fighters head back to and land on their respective carriers. There were thousands of fighters in the air for the battle, so it takes a little over an hour to get them back aboard the carriers. When the last fighter is finally aboard, the CAG gives Admiral Daniels a thumbs up to let him know he can get underway.

Admiral Daniels says, "Comms, send a message to all commands. Tell them to form up on the Valiant again, remind them of the seven point five kilometer radius and to use their thrusters and to move slowly and carefully so we don't have any collisions."

"Aye sir."

The communications officer sends the message and a few minutes later reports, "Admiral, all commands have acknowledged and are under way."

"Thank you, Comms."

He walks over to the port side bridge windows and sees the battle carrier Intrepid side slipping closer and closer until a person could almost step from one flight deck to the other.

On his police cruiser Nathan says, "We better get back aboard the Valiant before the fleet surrounds her. Ms. Arnoult, contact Valiant's air traffic control and request permission for a vertical landing on the elevator for shuttle bay alpha."

"Aye Captain."

A few moments later, Desiree says, "Captain, Valiant air traffic control has granted us clearance for a vertical landing on the elevator for shuttle bay alpha."

"Thank you, Ms. Arnoult."

"Mr. Bell?"

"Yes Captain?"

"You heard the lady, put her down on elevator for shuttle bay alpha."

"Aye Captain."

Mr. Bell fires up the sub-light engines and then nudges the throttles up. He slowly circles the ship around, lines her up, lowers the landing gear, and sets the ship down gently in the center of the massive elevator. After that he shuts down the engines. Ten seconds later the red strobe lights surrounding the elevator light up and rotate. The atmospheric force field activates, and the elevator starts to lower the police cruiser into the shuttle bay. As the tail of the police cruiser clears the flight deck, the huge shuttle bay doors above them begin to close. The crew looks out into the massive shuttle bay and the flurry of activity below them.

When the elevator reaches the deck, Nathan gets out of his chair and says, "Okay everyone, shut everything down and let's go."

The crew all answer in unison, "Aye Captain."

They get to work shutting all the ship's systems down. When finished, they all get up and follow Nathan down to the lower bay. Nathan opens the ramp and they walk out into the shuttle bay.

Nathan approaches the ground crew chief and says, "We'll be taking off again after we get back to our own time, so is it okay to leave our ship on the elevator?"

The ground crew chief gives Nathan the thumbs up and says, "You bet, sir."

Nathan pats him on the back and says, "Thanks, Chief."

He then turns to his crew and says, "Okay, let's head up to the bridge for the time jump."

Nathan and his crew take the tram and the elevator up to the bridge, Admiral Daniels meets Nathan just inside the large bridge doors.

The admiral shakes Nathan's hand and says, "Congratulations, Captain, your plan worked perfectly. I wish I could have seen Creeksto's face when he realized he failed."

Nathan smiles and says, "Thank you, Admiral, but I can't take all the credit. Everyone present played a part in the success of this mission."

"Always the modest one, Captain Stone."

"Yes sir. With your permission, Admiral, we would like to observe the time jump from the bridge then collect our prisoner and be on our way."

"Absolutely, Captain Stone, be my guest."

Nathan and his crew walk over to the port bridge windows and watch the ships maneuvering into formation. It takes about an hour for all the ships to get into position. Once again, the fleet looks like a massive steel ball, fifteen kilometers across, floating in space. When all ships have reported that they are ready, Admiral Daniels walks over to the control console for the time machine and powers it on. Once again, he follows the instructions the lead scientist gave him and checks to make sure that every part of every ship will be inside the bubble. The system gives him a green light, indicating that every ship will be inside the bubble when it forms. Next, he sets the date and time to jump forward to into the control console. He sets it so they will return one minute after they left. All that's left to do is press the execute button.

"Comms, open a channel to the fleet."

"Aye sir, channel open."

"Attention all commands, this is Admiral Daniels on the Valiant. We are ready to execute the time jump. I've set the return time to one minute after we left. Daniels out."

Admiral Daniels pushes the execute button, and just as before, the reactor's power output levels climb as the device starts to form the large time bubble around the fleet. The display on the control console shows a graphic of the bubble forming around the fleet, and a power monitoring graph which is climbing quickly towards one hundred percent.

When the graph reaches ninety-five percent Admiral Daniels says, "Time jump in 5… 4… 3… 2… 1… now."

The graph hits one hundred percent, there is a momentary flash of bright white light, and then the power levels drop quickly to zero as the bubble collapses.

Admiral Daniels asks, "Did it work? Did we jump back to our own time?"

The navigator says, "Affirmative sir. The other fleet disappeared, the Earth is almost one solar day away from us, and Earth's satellites' chronographs confirm we're back in our own time."

The bridge crew cheers.

Admiral Daniels smiles and says, "Hot damn. Comms, send a message to all commands. Tell them we're home. Disperse the fleet."

"Aye sir."

Soon after the communications officer sends the message, ships on the outer edge of the ball begin to peel off and spread out. Again, it takes about half an hour for all the ships in the fleet to disperse.

After watching the other battle carriers turn and move away from the Valiant, Admiral Daniels says, "Helm, plot a course for Earth. Take us home."

"Aye sir, plotting a course for Earth."

The battle carrier's sub-light engines ignite, the huge ship turns, and soon the Earth appears in the forward bridge windows. The rest of the fleet turns to follow the Valiant and before too long the fleet enters orbit around the shimmering blue ball, they call home.

Admiral Daniels walks over to the port bridge windows and looks down on the Earth. He sees North American and the sun reflecting off both the Pacific and Atlantic oceans.

He thinks to himself, "Home safe and sound and everything is right with the world."

Nathan walks over to Admiral Daniels, shakes his hand and says, "Thank you for everything, Admiral."

"No, Captain Stone, thank you."

Nathan turns to walk away when Admiral Daniels says, "Oh, Captain Stone..."

Nathan turns and says, "Yes, Admiral?"

"I'll have the Marine guard bring your prisoner, they'll have him there by the time you get to your ship."

"Thank you, Admiral, I appreciate it."

Nathan and his crew exit the bridge, take an elevator down to the carrier's internal tram and take a tram to shuttle bay alpha.

As promised, when they get to their ship, the Marine guard has Mr. Haggerty there waiting for them.

Mr. Black shows the Marines where the holding cells are in the lower bay of the police cruiser and they secure him in a cell for the trip down to Earth.

Nathan thanks the Marines and closes the ramp after they leave the ship. Then he and the rest of his crew head up to the bridge and take their seats.

The massive elevator rises, lifting the police cruiser up towards the flight deck. When the elevator is about half way to the flight deck, the atmospheric force field activates, and the elevator doors open. When the elevator reaches the flight deck, the crew hears a dull metallic thud.

Nathan says, "Ms. Arnoult, contact Valiant air traffic control and request clearance for a vertical takeoff."

"Aye Captain."

A few moments later Desiree says, "Captain, Valiant air traffic control says clearance for a vertical takeoff is granted, no traffic in the immediate area."

"Thank you, Ms. Arnoult."

"Mr. Bell?"

Mr. Bell turns to look at Nathan and says, "Yes, Captain?"

"Take us home."

Mr. Bell smiles and says, "Aye Captain."

He turns back around and begins the takeoff procedures.

On the outside of the ship, the diverters lower and the vertical takeoff vents open directing the thrust from the sub-light engines down towards the ground. Mr. Bell grabs the throttles with his right hand and slowly pushes them forward, increasing the power until the ship rises. When the ship reaches two hundred feet, Mr. Bell hits a button and the ship's systems adjust the diverters and vents to change from vertical takeoff to flight mode. The nose of the ship comes up slightly and the ship starts to move forward.

Mr. Bell retracts the landing gear and then says, "Hold on to your butts."

He grabs the throttles and rams them wide open causing the ship to accelerate rapidly, pushing the crew back in their seats.

Everyone on the bridge is smiling while watching Mr. Bell in his element.

When the ship clears the end of the massive battle carrier's flight deck, Mr. Bell turns and rolls the ship to port, and starts his descent towards Earth.

Nathan says, "Ms. Arnoult, contact Earth space flight control and request clearance for re-entry."

"Aye Captain."

A minute later Desiree says, "Captain, Earth space flight control has granted us clearance for re-entry, no traffic in the immediate area."

"Thank you, Ms. Arnoult."

"Mr. Black, plot a course to Seattle."

"Aye Captain, course laid in."

"Mr. Bell, take us to Seattle."

"Aye Captain."

As their ship approaches Seattle, Nathan says, "Ms. Arnoult, contact Seattle air traffic control, request an approach vector and clearance for a vertical landing at the Planetary Police headquarters helipad."

"Aye Captain."

A minute later Ms. Arnoult says, "Captain, Seattle air traffic control has cleared us for a vertical landing at the Planetary Police headquarters helipad and has sent me the approach vector. I have sent the approach vector to Mr. Black's console."

"Thank you, Ms. Arnoult."

Mr. Black reviews the data and says, "Confirmed, approach vector laid in, Captain."

"Thank you, Mr. Black."

"Mr. Bell, take us down."

"Aye Captain."

Mr. Bell pulls back on the throttles, the ship descends, they break through the clouds and the vast city that is Seattle comes into view. As they approach Planetary Police headquarters, Mr. Bell slows the ship down to a crawl and lines it up with the helipad. Soon the ship is hovering at two hundred feet directly over the helipad. Mr. Bell pulls back on the throttles a little more and the ship descends slowly. When the ship reaches fifty feet, the landing gear comes down. Moments later the wheels touch the ground and Mr. Bell shuts the engines down.

"Nice smooth landing as always, Mr. Bell."

"Thank you, Captain."

The crew finishes powering down the ship and then make their way from the bridge down to the lower bay. Nathan opens the ramp, and the crew walks out onto the helipad.

The ground crew is busy putting the chocks around the landing gear.

Nathan sees Carter standing, with the help of a set of crutches, at the edge of the helipad along with four other police officers.

Nathan and his crew walk over to see Carter and in true best friend fashion, Nathan smiles, shakes Carter's hand and says, "Are you still milking this injury thing? You can drop the act anytime we all know you're faking it. I mean seriously, crutches? You're taking it a little too far."

Everyone laughs and then Carter asks, "How did things go?"

Nathan looks around at his crew then back at Carter and says, "Oh just great, pretty routine really. You know, almost eaten by fire-breathing dragon worms on a desert planet, saw the Earth destroyed when the Sulari slammed the moon into the planet, went back in time and stopped that from happening. You know, that kind of thing. You can read all about it when I file my report in a few days."

Carter has a stunned look on his face and doesn't know if his friend is serious or pulling his leg.

All Carter can say is, "Ooooookay then, I look forward to your report."

Then Nathan points back over his shoulder with his thumb and says, "Oh yeah, I've got your old buddy Haggerty cooling his heels in a holding cell. If you want to take him off my hands, be my guest."

Carter looks at one of the other police officers and motions with his head towards Nathan's cruiser. The four officers head up the ramp into the lower bay of the police cruiser and return after a few minutes with Haggerty in hand cuffs.

As they pass by Carter says, "Welcome back, Marcus, I hope you enjoyed your little outing, it was the last one you will ever have."

Haggerty looks over his shoulder at Carter and gives him a dirty look but says nothing.

Carter says, "Geez that guy never shuts up, does he?"

"Yeah, he's a real blabbermouth."

Carter asks, "Heading home to Jasper now?"

"Yeah, we need a break. Our boss is such a slave driver."

Nathan turns and starts walking back towards his cruiser.

Carter chuckles and says, "Okay I'll come see you in a few days. Make sure you have lots of cold beer in the fridge."

Nathan turns back for a second, holds his arms straight out from his shoulders and says, "How many times do I have to remind you, I'm Canadian? We always have cold beer in the fridge."

Carter laughs and says, "See you soon."

Nathan waves to his friend as he turns to head up the ramp into the lower bay of the ship. His crew follows him in, and they close the ramp behind them.

Carter watches the ground crew pull the wheel chocks out of the way as the cruiser's jet engines wind up.

Nathan waves at Carter from the bridge windows as the ship's power comes on and the ship lifts off the helipad.

Carter waves back and watches the ship rise and take off across the sky to the north east. When the ship is out of sight Carter hobbles back inside police headquarters.

CHAPTER 17 – HOME SWEET HOME

After a forty-five minute flight, Nathan's ship is approaching his home in Jasper. They are flying slow and low, taking in the beauty of the Canadian Rocky Mountains, and the thick forest of trees that fills the valley and surrounds Nathan's home. Nathan activates the main viewscreen and sets it in split screen mode displaying the cameras on the bottom of the ship.

On the valley floor they see several moose, a mother grizzly bear and two cubs, a herd of whitetail deer and a herd of elk grazing lazily in the tall grass beside the river. It's a beautiful sunny afternoon in Jasper and the animals are out enjoying the nice weather.

Each member of Nathan's crew has a smile on their face watching the animals, not even realizing that they saved them as well. Sometimes we forget that we are not the only ones on the planet.

When they reach Nathan's home, Mr. Bell sets the ship down on the helipad and powers the engines down. The crew shuts down all the ship's systems and then make their way down to the lower bay. Nathan opens the ramp and they all walk out onto the helipad. Nathan pauses for a moment to close his eyes and breathe in deeply, smelling that fresh mountain air.

Desiree looks at Nathan and smiles watching him perform this ritual for she knows he is happiest when he is at his home in the mountains. She walks over and takes his hand and they follow the rest of the crew up to the house.

There isn't much food in the house, so Nathan and Desiree grab the keys for his second favorite car, which is his 1970 plum crazy purple Hemi Cuda convertible, and head into town to buy some groceries.

Being a gentleman Nathan opens the door for Desiree so she can get in, then he walks around to the driver's side and gets in. Nathan starts the car up and revs that mean sounding hemi a few times, making Desiree smile. Nathan pulls the car out of the garage and drops the top so they can really enjoy the view as they drive through the mountains.

When they drive into Jasper, many people walking on the main street stop and stare at the antique car as it drives by. Just like Nathan's 1969 Camaro Z28, the Cuda gets a lot of peoples' attention when he brings it in to town.

Nathan and Desiree buy a whole car full of groceries, beer, scotch, and a few bottles of champagne to celebrate the success of their first mission as a team. And what a mission it was.

They started out chasing a team of felons down and ended up being key players in saving the Earth from being destroyed, the human race from annihilation, and they were also among the first humans to experience time travel. It was quite a week.

When they are done their shopping, they drive back to Nathan's house, unload the groceries, and put the Cuda back in the garage. They find the rest of the crew relaxing on the deck out back enjoying a few ice-cold beers and discussing parts of the mission. When Nathan and Desiree walk out onto the deck, the crew is ribbing Mr. Black about getting slimed twice while wearing the exo-suit. He now knows he will never live that down.

Nathan is carrying a couple bottles of the champagne they just bought, and Desiree is carrying six champagne flutes. They set everything down on the large patio table and invite everyone to join them.

The crew gathers around Nathan as he pops the first bottle open and says, "Tonight, we celebrate the success of our first mission as a team."

He fills up all six glasses and hands them out while continuing on, "A mission that started out running down an escaped felon, but then took a slight jog to the left," the crew chuckles, "and we end up in an all-out battle to save our world."

Nathan raises his glass slightly and says, "The first toast tonight is to you. You all performed admirably throughout the entire mission. You kept your heads under pressure, even after witnessing the Earth's destruction, we caught the bad guy, and helped save the planet. As your captain, I couldn't be happier or prouder."

Nathan raises his glass higher and says, "To the best damned crew in the Planetary Police."

The crew all cheer, "Here, here," clink their glasses together, and take a drink.

Mr. Black then holds up his glass and says, "Here's to Nathan Stone, the best damned captain in the Planetary Police, and a brilliant tactician whose battle plan saved the planet from destruction."

The crew all cheer, "Here here," clink their glasses together and take another drink.

When they finish their champagne, Nathan fires up the barbecue and the crew starts to prepare their dinner. Nathan turns the stereo up loud, blasting some classic rock music before bringing out a beer for every member of the crew. When dinner is ready, the crew feasts out on the deck. When they can't eat any more, they clean up and head inside to relax and watch an old science fiction movie before retiring for the night.

Everyone was up late so the next morning everyone sleeps in. Nathan wakes at 10:30 hours to find Desiree still in a very deep sleep. Nathan decides to let her sleep, so he quietly slips out of bed, goes into the kitchen to make some coffee, then heads into his office to file his mission report.

A little later on that day, Nathan is outside backing the police cruiser into his hangar using the tug vehicle, when he hears a helijet approaching. He looks up just as it clears the trees and descends onto his helipad. The rest of the crew comes out of the hangar to see what the noise is. When the helijet lands Carter gets out with his crutches and hobbles towards them. The helijet lifts off again, climbs straight up, takes off across the sky and is soon out of sight. Nathan shuts the engine off on the tug, jumps down and walks towards Carter.

"Hey buddy, what are you doing here?

Carter looks at Nathan in disbelief, holds up a tablet and says, "We need to talk about the mission report you filed."

"Oh? What about it?"

Just then the group hears another ship approaching and they look up with curiosity. This time it's a fairly large military transport ship that flies in just above the trees and descends onto the helipad. Everyone stands there watching, as the rear ramp of the transport ship opens, wondering who will come out. They don't have to wait long for as soon as the ramp hits the ground Secretary of the Fleet, Admiral Hollister walks down the ramp, out of the ship, and over to where Carter and Nathan are standing.

Nathan reaches out, shakes his hand and says, "Good morning, Admiral Hollister, this is a pleasant surprise."

Nathan motions towards Carter and says, "Admiral, you remember Captain Carter Rayburn of the Planetary Police force."

Admiral Hollister reaches out, shakes Carter's hand and says, "Yes, it's a pleasure to see you again, Captain Rayburn."

Admiral Hollister looks back at Nathan and says, "Captain Stone, I came here to thank you for the role you played in defeating the Sulari and saving the planet. Your tactical plan was brilliantly effective and kept our casualties to a minimum."

"Thank you, Admiral."

Admiral Hollister continues, "I also wanted to tell you that the world council has decided that time travel is too dangerous to play around with, so the time machine is being removed from the Valiant and will be hidden away in an undisclosed super-secret military storage facility."

"The council also decided that every piece of the Trynx 3 ore will be recovered and returned to the planet, and that a permanent military presence will be established there in the form of a battle group, a military space station and a web of defense satellites, to ensure that no one else gets their hands on any of that ore."

"Even if the Sulari managed to get their hands on the ore they weren't smart enough to create a time machine on their own. Someone else had to be building the time machine for them."

Nathan says, "I agree, but who, Admiral?"

"We have no way of knowing, we'll just have to wait for them to reveal themselves. I don't think we've heard the last of this."

"Agreed, Admiral."

"Now for the second reason for my visit, I believe you have three crates of that very ore aboard your police cruiser, Captain Stone. I will take it off your hands and make sure it's sent back to Trynx 3."

"Of course, Admiral."

Nathan turns to look at his crew and says, "Mr. Bell, Mr. Black, would you grab the three crates of the Trynx 3 ore from our ship and load them onto the admiral's transport?"

Mr. Bell and Mr. Black both answer in unison, "Aye Captain."

Both men then head over to the police cruiser in the hangar, open the lower bay ramp, and walk inside.

Carter raises his hand holding the tablet that contains Nathan's mission report and says, "So this... this really happened?"

Nathan says, "Yes, yes it did."

Carter looks at Admiral Hollister who simply raises his eyebrows and nods his head.

Carter looks stunned.

Mr. Bell and Mr. Black walk past carrying the three crates of ore and take them up the ramp into the admiral's transport. They set them down and walk back down the ramp and out of the transport.

As they walk back past them Nathan says, "Thank you, gentlemen."

The admiral reaches out to shake Nathan's hand and says, "Thank you, Captain Stone, it's always a pleasure."

Nathan says, "Likewise, Admiral."

The Admiral turns to Carter, reaches out to shake his hand and says, "Nice to see you again, Captain Rayburn."

Carter says, "Nice to see you again, Admiral."

The admiral turns and walks back over to his transport, up the ramp and inside the ship. The ramp raises, and the engines spin up. When the engines have fully started, the power comes on, the ship lifts off, straight up above the trees, and then takes off across the sky.

Nathan looks at Carter and says, "You look like you could use a beer. Come on, we'll tell you all about it."

Carter says, "I have a feeling I'm going to need something stronger than beer for this one."

Nathan motions to his crew and says, "Come on everyone, we'll fill Carter in on everything over a few beers."

The crew heads towards Nathan and Carter. Nathan puts his arm around Desiree as they walk up to the house and go inside.

Just as Nathan and Desiree are going through the door Nathan laughs and says, "Wait until you hear how Mr. Black got slimed twice."

Carter pauses, turns back and smiles at Mr. Black who is walking just behind him and says, "Oh, I can't wait to hear this."

Mr. Black smiles, shakes his head, walks past Carter into the house and says, "I'm never going to live that down."

Carter laughs, hobbles into the house on his crutches and closes the door behind him.

THE END

GLOSSARY

CAG – this is an acronym for Commander, Air Group. The CAG is responsible for all the embarked squadrons, their aircraft and their personnel aboard a battle carrier.

FTL – this is an acronym for "faster than light" and in this book refers to the fact that a ship is traveling faster than the speed of light and also to the engines / drive that propels a ship to speeds faster than the speed of light.

TSL – this is an acronym for "times the speed of light" and in this book is a reference to the speed a ship is traveling at. In several instances in this book you will see a ship's speed referred to as 14 TSL which is the top speed achieved by the latest and greatest FTL drive so far. It reads as 14 times the speed of light, but that is not quite accurate. The actual speed is 14^3 X the speed of light or 14 X 14 X 14 X the speed of light.

VTOL – this is an acronym for "vertical takeoff and landing" which means a ship equipped for this can take off and land without a runway very much like a helicopter. The British Harrier jump jet and the American F-35 fighter are current examples of VTOL capable fighters.

<u>DID YOU ENJOY THIS STORY?</u>

If you answered yes to the question above, I would appreciate it if you could spend a couple of minutes and leave a review on the book's page wherever you bought it. I am a new author, this is the first book I have published, and positive reviews of my book will help bring it to the attention of other readers.

You can see my other titles at: **seanpatrickposey.com**

ABOUT THE AUTHOR

Sean Patrick Posey was born in Edmonton, Alberta, Canada in August of 1969 to parents Dave and Margaret Posey. Sean has two older brothers named Mark and Todd. Sean was hooked on science fiction at an early age. Some of his favorites include:

- Star Trek (TOS)
- Star Wars (original trilogy)
- Battlestar Galactica (TOS)
- Alien and Aliens
- Stargate Atlantis

Some of his other interests include classic 60s and 70s muscle cars, camping, fishing, martial arts, 3D computer animation and modeling, weight lifting and technology.

Sean graduated from the Northern Alberta Institute of Technology (NAIT) in 1992 earning his diploma in Computer Engineering Technology and has been an I.T. person for the last 27 years specializing in network design, installation and support.

Sean has two beautiful daughters from his first marriage named Alyssa and Sarah whom he loves dearly.

In January of 2017 he married the love of his life Nicole Hayman. Nicole is an American born in Los Angeles, but was living in St. Charles, Missouri when the couple met online. They spent 7 years in a long distance relationship before marrying and Nicole has now moved up to Edmonton to live with Sean. Nicole encouraged Sean to write this first book.

Printed in Great Britain
by Amazon